SNAKE
Nest of Vipers

AIRSHIP 27 PRODUCTIONS

Snake: Nest of Vipers
© 2015 Michael Lail
An Airship 27 Production

Editor: Ron Fortier
Associate Editor: Peg Livingston
Cover illustrations © 2015 Ted Hammond
Interior illustrations © copyright 2015 Greg Keyzer
Production and design by Rob Davis
Marketing and Promotions Manager: Michael Vance

Published by Airship 27 Productions
airship27hangar.com

ISBN-13: 978-0692406472 (Airship 27)
ISBN-10: 0692406476

Printed in the United States of America

10 9 8 7 6 5 4 3 2 1

by Michael Vance

from an unpublished and uncopyrighted
premise by comics pioneer Richard E. Hughes

"What infinite use Dante would have made of the Bowery."
—Theodore Roosevelt, 1914
Special thanks to Wayne Downing for historical references

Chapter One

espite what the self-crowned 'deep thinkers' say, there has never been a time when nothing existed.

Nothing existing is a contradiction, an oxymoron, an impossibility.

In fact, even nature hates a vacuum and will fill it with a cliche if necessary.

One such cliche is that there are only two types of people, those who see a glass as half full and those who see a glass as half empty.

The vacuum filled with this cliche is the empty space in the skull of any idiot who cannot see that a glass must be half full <u>and</u> half empty at the same time.

If this is true, and it is with a vengeance, and I know it is, then why do I feel so horribly and utterly... empty.

July 1951, Bowery, New York City

It was a nasty night. But I suppose that most nights are nasty in the Bowery.

It was dark as pitch and past midnight when the three thieves came out of the back of the pawn shop into the alley trying to be invisible. One carried a small attaché case, one a bag like doctors carry in old cowboy movies, and all wore ski masks and jackets. There was a hot, stiff wind blowing the litter in the alley around like cockroaches that scatter when someone turns on a light switch in a flophouse, and, boy, are there a lot of those in the Bowery. Flophouses and cockroaches—the insect and human kind. The one utility pole at the mouth of the alley shed only a feeble halo of light from its bulb, and the sky was a blanket of clouds heavy with rain.

They—the crooks—came out of the back door into the alley quickly and started to walk briskly from the pawn shop that was the middle shop of about ten businesses. Their heels clicked on the asphalt like little firecrackers exploding. They made it about ten steps towards the mouth of the alley and a clean get-a-way when they saw her.

The thief with the doctor's bag said, "Damn," under his breath. Well, I didn't actually hear that, but it's a good guess.

She stood with her legs spread apart like ramparts in the middle of the alley ahead of the thugs, blocking their escape. She wore a big, black, unbuttoned overcoat that fell to her ankles and that, occasionally, was whipped open and to her sides by the wind. That let them know she was a she. It only took a second for the thieves to take all of this in.

When they saw her, it was like she was talking to someone who wasn't there. She said in a voice like the hiss of a snake, "When this is over, my friend, they'll be no need for me to come again."

While they were trying to figure out what that meant, she put her balled fists on her ample hips, tipped back her head a little, and laughed like a man.

She had a body that makes men ache and everything she wore was leather. Her torso was needlessly accented by a dark blue kind of thing slightly open between her headlights—I mean, her breasts— and held closed by leather draw strings. Leather flames of a slightly lighter blue rose up from her waist and spread to her ribs and what looked like fish or snake scales were embossed in the bustier. Yeah. That's it. It's called a boos-t-ay. Leather armlets that covered her forearms up to but just short of her elbows were also laced closed. Her black leather tights ended in boots that ended just above her calves.

In her left hand, she held a quarterstaff easily five feet long topped by something indistinguishable in the dark. I learned later what it was. On her left hip was attached a coiled blacksnake whip. Her long, brown hair, restless in the breeze, danced like leaves blown in the wind around the tops of her breasts.

The mask she wore was enough to stop any man in his tracks. Her face was hidden by an expressionless, almond smooth, Kabuki mask with a cobra coiled around her left eye down her cheek to the tip of her chin.

This would have stopped any man dead to rights, but these three were not just any man, and the thief with the attaché case began to reach inside his jacket with his free hand as he took three steps towards her.

"Welcome to Sherwood, my lads," said the crazy broad. "A lie can travel halfway around the world while the truth is putting on its shoes."

"Are you nuts or something?" said the thief as he continued to walk with deadly determination towards her. "Who the Hell you think *you* are? Errol Flynn?"

The woman tossed the quarterstaff she held in her right hand to her left hand.

"What a pity her manners," she said as she raised her right arm parallel to her body, "don't match her looks."

The thief said, "Ulp," stopped in his tracks, and staggered two steps back. He looked down and saw a dart embedded in his chest near his heart. He looked up and saw the right arm of the staff she extended with two fingers pressed into the palm of her hand.

"Be careful," she said, "about reading health books. You may die of a misprint."

He fell face forward on the asphalt, spasmed once, and lay still.

Oblivious to this, and still determined to remove the obstacle to their planned getaway and a future life of ease and debauchery for at least a month or two, the other two thieves broke into what was intended to be an end run around her.

Nonplused, she said, "I like my whiskey old and my women young."

In two heartbeats, three things happened at almost the same time.

The two thieves reached either side of the crazy broad.

Balanced on her left leg, the she kicked out. It's not like in the movies. You can't really hear a bone break, but she broke the kneecap of the thief on her right side with the doctor's bag and he fell with a sharp yelp several feet away from her.

The remaining thief on her right side and just a little beyond her broke into a broken-field run like a quarterback in football.

It doesn't take long to cover thirty yards or so when someone is scared out of their wits, and that kind of person is focused on only one thing, staying alive.

It was then the third thing happened. The bum—that would be me—began to walk across the mouth of the alley just beneath that utility pole in front of the thief with the woman trotting at her ease close behind him. I'd just left *McGurk's Suicide Hall* just down the street. For those who have never been to the Bowery—the blest among men—that's a bar.

I turned at the sound of running feet just as the thief tackled me, knocking both of us off of our feet and knocking my cane out of my hand sending it spinning several feet away down the sidewalk. He knocked my hat off and the cigarette out of my mouth -the last Camel I had. Now, all of the rest of this, I experienced myself.

On the ground and with one arm around my neck, the thief drew a gun out of his jacket. He pressed the cold barrel of the forty-five against my head behind my left ear as the woman in leather arrived.

Just then, it thundered big and began to spit cold rain.

He said, "Take one step closer, and I'll blow his brains out."

He had no time to hear an answer and she never offered one. Before the last word was out of his mouth, the quarterstaff had come up and smashed down on the side of this head just above his ear.

There was the smell of blood and Brylcreem. His body went limp. His hand relaxed and the gun fell out of it onto the asphalt. It began to rain a bit harder.

Looking at me, the woman said, "Who are *you*, my pretty?"

The words were distorted by the Kabuki mask, making it sound like a snake hissed them, but I could tell she had a slight German accent.

"I'm James Bridges, but everybody calls me Admiral," I said, sitting up.

"Why Admiral?"

"'Cause someday my ship will come in," I said as I searched for and found my cane in the darkness.

"This is his and your lucky day, Admiral. *He* isn't dead, just knocked unconscious. Feel this."

She stuck the head of her quarterstaff down by my cane, and I wasn't in any position to argue about it so I reached up and felt it. That's when I learned what was there. It felt like a hard rubber, like a rubber mallet, not like metal, and like the head of a cobra with its mouth open and its fangs showing.

"And *you* aren't dead either. That's because I'm not Jack the Ripper tonight."

"I'd feel even luckier if you were Jesus tonight."

It thundered again, and the rain began to fall heavier, so I pulled up my collar around my neck.

"It's cold tonight," she hissed. "What are you doing out?"

She threw a snow of business cards on the clubbed thief, each picturing a cobra—one of those hooded snakes—poised to strike.

I didn't answer. As I started to get up off of the sidewalk, I said: "Th' cops aren't gonna believe this. Who do I say you are?"

She said, "It isn't what they say about you, it's what they whisper."

I said, "What?"

Snake told me almost all of this two days later in the Bowery flophouse where I lived at the time—the Sunshine Hotel—when I could afford what they call a room. Yeah, even the part about her body. She told me again in her rooms in the flophouse in the Bowery where we've lived for the last two years. She told me the first time because I didn't see most of it.

You see, I'm blind.

August 1951, Bowery, New York City

The beefy, red-knuckled hand snatched with the sound of a slap and held fast the john's raised fist before he could strike again.

"Hey!" the sloshed bucket of fury barked and turned his sotted face to find the owner of the hand who held him. He found her. His leer twisted into a question mark. "Wha' are ya doin', Mary. I paid up?"

She was built like a wooden beer keg dressed in a floral shift. Her brown hair was cut short like a man's crewcut, her lips were ruby red, her cheeks were heavily roughed, and her bared, uneven teeth were brown from tobacco stains. The thought flashed through the drunk's mind that no dame, even one built like a side of beef, could stop him.

"No one hits one of mine, not tonight," snarled Typhoid Mary, her eyes slits and her jaw set for murder. "Not ever."

She jerked the john back who, stripped to the waist, was so hairy that he looked like a bear with a bad case of mange. She jerked him partially up from the bed where the crumpled cotton sheet barely covered the nakedness of one of her girls cringing there, sobbing, with a blackened eye.

"Who the Hell do you think you are," the john snarled, his voice low and threatening, and jerked his hand free. He stood up on the mattress on unsteady legs.

"Who?" mocked Mary. "Who?"

The girl on the bed snatched the sheet up in an instinctive modesty to cover her nakedness. It seemed a silly thing to do, even to her and certainly to Typhoid; most of the framed prints and calendars that decorated the wallpaper were of naked or near naked women. But she did it instinctively, without thought.

"This is who. I'm the Hell you think I am, Johnnie," said Mary in a dead monotone, and shoved him hard with both of her paws flat on his naked chest.

He stumbled back and fell off of the mattress. He staggered up on unsteady, naked feet, and stumbled back two steps against a small, Formica topped end table. A plain lamp with a Hop-a-long Cassidy shade on the cheap table rocked back and forth and the shallow bowl next to a damp washcloth threw up water from the impact.

The john lunged around the bed at Mary. She sidestepped him, and shoved him again, both hands on his hairy, flabby back. Thrown forward by his momentum and her strength and unable to check his steps that had now become a brief and ill-destined trot from the force of her shove, he struck the wall next to the open door of the whore's room.

"Get out and stay out," Mary said flatly.

"No damn skirt...."

Typhoid Mary was on him before he could shake the effects of the impact from his groggy head. She grabbed him by the belt that cinched up his dungarees and his right shoulder, swung him around, and shoved him through the open door into the hallway of Mother Mary's Lonely Hearts Club, her brothel.

"That means don't ever come back," she growled.

Before the john could recover his balance, she pushed him again, hard, down the hallway to the mouth of the stairwell that lead to the second of three floors of Typhoid's brothel. She followed him as he stumbled backward, striking the railing, grabbing it, and partially straightening.

Below them, in a small lobby that looked more like a living room with frayed carpeting, overstuffed furniture, garish lamps, and cheap framed prints on the wallpapered walls, overstuffed men in various stages of arousal and drunkenness and under-dressed women involved in the eternal dance meant to make babies all looked up in unison to the top of the stairs. A tall, thin man dressed like a cheap burlesque magician in a tattered suit with tails and a top hat sat at a piano playing a ragtime tune. He looked over his shoulder as his fingers danced over the keys and winked at Mary and her victim.

It had long been rumored that the drunk who'd given Mary her distinctive nickname years earlier had meant to call her Typhoon Mary and slurred that into Typhoid. The john at the top of the stairs learned why typhoon fit her better.

She pushed him down the stairwell.

He fought to find purchase on the railing or the wall or even on the stairs themselves as he clutched with both hands at anything and nothing to save himself, but he found no anchor. Randomly striking the railing and the wall like the steel ball in a pinball machine as he fell in a bizarre blizzard of flailing limbs, he tumbled down, screaming, with Mary resolutely following him down on the stairs.

Literally and figuratively, he hit bottom with a bone-wrenching thud and an exhalation of breath.

Mary was on him before he could rise from the foot of the stairwell, grabbing him by the hair and the seat of his pants, and dragging him the short distance to the front door of her brothel. She dropped him on the floor, threw open the door, picked him up by his hair and butt again, and threw him out.

Typhoid Mary slammed the door, shot a glance that would kill a charging lion over her left shoulder at her guests and hostesses behind her, and turned around to her right side.

Grinning, an old black man in sunglasses stood before her.

"Now what the Hell do *you* want, Admiral" she demanded, her face still flushed with blood and pink from her anger and exertion.

The old black man smiled, touched the lower edge of his sunglasses, and handed something to Mary.

Mary looked down.

The card in her palm bore the image of a striking cobra.

The little desk in her cubicle was an organized chaos of four small, index-card file cabinets, four black phones (one was mounted on the wall), a desk calendar full of xed-out dates, and an accordion bracket that, like an extended arm ending in a fist, ended in a microphone that jutted only inches from her face.

Amy Smith was also an organized chaos. Her police uniform of a starched, off-white, long-sleeved blouse decorated with the appropriate police badges and stripes and her dark-blue, pleated khaki pants spoke of a neatness that hid a disaster of a life.

It was that disaster, a recent divorce that had left her and her five year old daughter hanging on the edge of abject poverty that Amy was thinking of as she sat down in front of her desk to begin another of more than one thousand mundane days as a police dispatcher in precinct nine in Gotham.

She was thirty one years old, with bleached blonde hair that did not make her look like Marilyn Monroe, despite her self-deception. Because about one-eighth of an inch of brown roots showed under the blonde, the faux coloring made her look like a snow-topped mountain peak. She had large, deep blue eyes, high cheek bones, flawless skin, full lips, and a heart-shaped jaw. Every man in the precinct wanted her. No man ever asked her out on a date. They all knew she had a kid.

Amy noticed the envelope on her desk almost immediately. She picked it up and glanced to her left to see if any of the other three dispatchers noticed. They did not. She saw that there was no stamp and no return address on the front of the envelope, just her typed name. She turned the envelope over; its surface was blank. She folded the envelope in two and palmed it.

"Nancy," she said to the dispatcher next to her who looked up on hearing her spoken name. "I need to hit the ladies room. Cover for me?"

Nancy Karlson nodded affirmatively.

In moments, Amy was closing the bathroom door behind her. She moved to a stall, and sat down. She unfolded the envelope and carefully tore in open along its sealed flap. She looked inside.

Amy Smith counted out three one hundred dollar bills, one at a time.

Behind the last bill was a business card with the image of a striking cobra.

August 1952, Manhattan, New York City

The '42 Plymouth DeSoto taxi that lurched to the curb had been a bright green at one time. The lettering on its passenger's side that spelled "Star Taxi Co." and was originally painted in a solid yellow now looked like an after-thought painted with dried mud. The taxi was a derelict, an embarrassment, and so was its cabbie, and the man waiting on the sidewalk stepped back instinctively as it stopped by the curb.

That he'd stepped back was more than enough to irritate his potential fare who took pride in not only understanding every aspect of the animal nature of human beings, but in being in control of those instincts and, therefore, capable of being somewhat objective in his reading of the common flotsam of New York City. He was, after all, a professional and tolerant of all deviations of the human condition.

He was dead wrong in his self-assessment.

That man on the Park Avenue sidewalk was huge at 6'4', weighed three-hundred pounds, and looked more like a stevedore, or lumberjack, or dockworker, or professional wrestler, or a member of a motorcycle gang than like Freud or Jung (as if anyone knew what Jung looked like), or like any other psychologist. But he was a psychologist, and a very successful one.

His brown hair was cropped short, he wore a Fu Manchu mustache that did not end at the line of his jaw but continued halfway down his throat, and a short-sleeved black shirt with two vertical, white strips that began at his shoulders and ended at his shirt tails that were not tucked into his beige khakis. Beneath the front of his shirt and tucked into the waist of his jeans was hidden a pearl handled revolver.

He also wore a pair of expensive sunglasses on top of his head and carried a folded newspaper under his left arm.

The back passenger's door was flung open by an unseen hand, and the waiting man bent forward and squatted a bit to see inside. Inside sat a wizened old black man on the bench seat behind an opaque glass partition separating him and an unseen driver. The old man was dressed in a second-hand, wrinkled suit like bums wear that had once been black, and still held the memory of a crease in the cuffed pants. His shoes where black, scuffed, heavy and cheap. He was wearing sun glasses, his close-cropped hair was peppered with gray, his mustache was unevenly trimmed, and he was sitting as if he were oblivious that the door was open. The psychologist took careful note of all of this because the police would want to know.

"Hello, I'm Doctor..." began the squatting man.

"Get in," interrupted the wrinkled black man without moving anything but his left hand to indicate that he was even alive.

The doctor got inside, closing the door as he sat down. Immediately, he noticed the old man who was now facing and smiling broadly at him, and the song on the radio, "Tell Me Why" by the Four Aces, that was muffled somewhat by the taxi's opaque glass partition.

The old man offered a folded handkerchief draped across the palm of his right hand to the doctor. "Put it on," he said, gesturing with his left hand. "Over your eyes."

"I don't see why that's necessary," said the doctor, accepting the handkerchief out of curiosity and a sense of politeness for the old.

"So you can be blind like me," added his host. The psychologist noted that he 'spoke' with his hands, accenting each of his words with a movement like a maestro uses a baton to direct an orchestra.

"Even if I put it on, what's to keep me from simply removing it? How would you know one way or the other?"

"Hank would know," said the black man, turning to face the back of the driver's seat again. "That ain't no privacy glass. It's a one-way mirror, and my man, Hank—he's the hack—can see every move you make. Put it on."

"I don't see..." the doctor began to object again.

"Put...it...on!" interrupted the black bum. "You've already seen me, and that's too much. Everybody that sees me just paints one more bullseye on my back, and I got too many of them there already. If you seen where we was going and who we are, it'd paint a bullseye on *your* back, and the Snake don't miss. So you sure as Hell ain't going to know where we're going."

"My name is Doctor Joseph Eacobacci," said the psychologist as he placed the cloth over his eyes and tied a knot in it at the back of his head. Only then did he realize that the old man didn't have the unclean smell of the bums of skid row.

"I already know that, doc. You can call me Admiral just like everyone else does. Now, sit back and shut up. You're on your way. You just don't know where you're going."

"That's clever, Admiral. That's what Stymie says in the *Our Gang* flickers."

"Nope," said the old black man with a finality that allowed no response. "That's what I says to someone who won't sit back and shut up."

It just didn't fit.

Except for two aluminum folding chairs with arm rests and a thin layer of dust on everything, the windowless room was otherwise empty of any furnishings of any kind. The psychologist's blindfold was draped over the arm of the chair where he sat.

Dr. Joseph Eacobacci didn't quite fit on the metal chair either. Yet he looked the standard for normalcy compared to the spectacular woman who glided into the room on the pads of her bare feet with a roll of her hips that told him she was not only aware of her sexuality, but celebrated its impact on men.

Except for me he said inside his head. But that was a lie.

Eacobacci pretended to ignore her as he studied a drawing of the woman dubbed Snake by the press in New York City that was printed next to the story above the fold of the *Tog Morgen Zhurnal,* the newspaper he'd brought with him. No Gotham newspaper photographer had been at the right time and place to snap an actual photograph of the leather-clad she-devil yet. Hence, the artist's sketch full of guesswork and imagination. In the drawing, Snake was bashing in the head of a thief with an ax. Eacobacci's belief that the drawing must be exaggerated wavered as he watched the woman dressed all in leather, with a whip coiled on her left hip stop in front of the chair opposite him.

She wore a dark blue bustier with leather flames rising on both sides of her chest. It was laced closed by leather draw strings. Leather armlets that covered her forearms were also laced closed. Her black tights ended at her bare ankles.

She did not carry a snake-headed quarterstaff. The dart mechanism was missing from her wrist. A Kabuki mask embellished with a cobra on its left side was tied over her face by yellow ribbon that disappeared at her temples underneath a head of tightly curled blonde hair. *Surely* he thought to himself, *this is an obvious cry for attention.*

The newspaper headline read: Seventh Criminal Clubbed by Mystery Vigilante. The smaller sub-headline read: Criminal's Loot Missing. A second sub-headline read: City Panics.

Eacobacci let the newspaper drop to his lap as the woman poured herself into the empty chair opposite him. She folded her left thigh over her right thigh and wiggled the toes of her naked left foot.

"You look a little shocked," she said in her distorted voice. "You must understand, I can't go back to yesterday because I was a different person then."

"What is that supposed to mean?"

"What part do you not understand about 'you look a little shocked'?"

"Oh, I get it. The newspaper said you talk in riddles. I can't say I'm shocked. If I may be so bold, in a world where children huddle under school desks to protect themselves from an A-bomb, the Soviet Union has three times as many airplanes as us, and four times the number of troops, flying saucers are peppering the night skies, and Betty Page is posing nude while she chews Beech Nut Chlorophyll Gum, I can't say a woman dressed as you do is particularly shocking, Miss....?"

"Puddintain. If you ask me again, I'll tell you the same."

"Let's try a different approach," said the doctor. "I'm glad that the Admiral was able to bring me to this meeting today."

"The Admiral? I don't know any... oh, you mean Mr. Bojangles, don't you." She reversed the position of her crossed legs. "We sing and dance together."

The woman in the chair opposite him leaned forward, presenting her breasts to the doctor. She whispered, "I don't really like him. He's black, you know. And blind."

"Yes, I know he's black and blind," answered Eacobacci. "I guess I got his name wrong. There was a lot of sleight-of-hand in getting here. I suspect all of the secrecy in getting here is just part of what I hope we can discuss tonight. I am Doctor Joseph Eacobacci. But you can call me Joey. I am a psychologist as well as the father of the little kidnapped girl you saved. What is your name?"

"Oh, my goodness," she giggled. "A shrink. I stopped believing in Santa Clause when I was six, doctor. Mother took me to see him in a department store, and he asked *me* for an autograph. Everybody knows me. I'm Shirley, silly," she continued with a German accent. "Shirley Temple."

Eacobacci held up the newspaper with a finger on the drawing and story about her for her to read.

"The reporters are calling you 'Snake' because of the bronze head of a snake on top of the quarterstaff you usually carry. This reporter, Leo Rosenbaum, who wrote this story for the Jewish newspaper in the Bowery, the *Tog Morgen Zhurnal*, wrote that one of the criminals you robbed said you must have been Liza Borden this time because of the ax you were swinging around like a madwoman and because you were chanting that nursery rhyme: "Lizzie Borden took an ax, and gave her mother forty whacks. When she saw what she had done, she gave her father forty-one.'"

"That's just silly," said Shirley. "I can't read and I'm not a snake and I don't have an ax, do I? I'm just a little girl."

"The story says that the man you clubbed unconscious begged for his life. It also says you randomly kill criminals and keep their loot for yourself."

"That's just a naughty lie," said the woman behind the inscrutable Kabuki mask. "When I was fourteen, I was the oldest I ever was. I've been getting younger ever since. Don't you agree, Santa dear?"

Eacobacci studied Snake for a moment before continuing to speak.

"I must admit, it does sound a little crazy." Eacobacci laid the paper on his lap without taking his eyes off of the woman. "Even this Leo fellow wrote that he couldn't confirm the axe thing.

"Be that as it may, I wanted to meet you for two reasons…Shirley. First, I wanted to thank you for saving my daughter's life and bringing her home to me. I'm told that at the time you rescued her you were pretending to be Judy Garland when she was Dorothy from the Wizard of Oz movie. Is that true?"

"I almost got that part," said Snake. "I would have been a great Dorothy, but they said I didn't sing good enough."

"Secondly, I think you may need my help. I'd like to know why you… pretend to be other people…and I'd like to get to know you and possibly find out why you steal from criminals. That's not considered normal behavior in my profession."

There was a long moment of uncanny silence but no movement from the woman in the chair.

"Did I say something to offend you, Shirley?" asked the doctor.

"Could you fix my dolly, doc. She's at home and has a broken neck."

"I'm not that kind of doctor, Shirley. I help people feel better when they are hurt inside, when they are sad or angry or confused about something. I'd like to help you because you helped my daughter."

"Oh," Shirley said, and her shoulders slumped a little. "I have never let my schooling interfere with my education. I like what you're wearing today, doctor."

"Thank you, Shirley. But, I…"

Snake leaned forward in her chair.

"Clothes make the man. But naked people have little or no influence on society."

"I think you just quoted Mark Twain, didn't you? Do you hide behind those quotes? Are you very sad or angry inside and that's why you hide behind words and hurt people, Shirley?"

There was another long moment of silence.

"You ask too many questions. Would you like me to sing 'Animal Crackers', doc?"

"Of course I would, but some other time. Did you hear my question, Shirley?"

"No."

"I asked why you hurt some people."

There was a third long moment of silence.

"I can't help you feel better inside unless you talk to me, Shirley."

"Oh, goodness," Snake answered, half-rising from her folding chair, "I think it's past my bed time. I have to go now, doc."

"So soon? Before you go," began Eacobacci, knowing even as he did so that the Kabuki mask would fulfill its purpose and hide her emotional response to his question, whether it be a smile, a grimace, a biting of lip, or even suppressed laughter, "I wonder…Shirley. Have you ever thought of…hurting me?"

There was no response; she did not even sit back down on the chair. The momentary silence in the room was oppressive.

"Are you even thinking of hurting me now?"

The woman in the Kabuki mask held up her hand to show her thumb and index finger almost touching.

"Well," she said, "maybe just a little."

Dr. Eacobacci picked up the handset of his black telephone, dialed a number, and leaned back in his tufted, brown leather chair behind his well organized mahogany desk that stood precisely two-thirds of the way back from and faced the paneled door to his office in Manhattan. His sun glasses lay next to the telephone cradle. Behind him, a large, plate-glass window gave him a wonderful view of the skyscrapers of New York City. As the telephone rang, he looked at his modest collection of lithographs hanging on his mahogany paneled walls of modern paintings by Jackson Pollack, Franz Kline, and Mark Rothko. Then his attention drifted to the little wooden bird at the right side and front edge of his desk that dipped its beak into a shot-glass full of water, then slowly jerked up, bobbed, then dipped again—a gag gift from his best friend meant to keep him "calm". Someone picked up the handset of the telephone on the other side of the line.

"Honey?" said Eacobacci. "It's me."

"Hello, sweetie! Is something wrong?"

"Of course not. I called because I'm between patients, and I have some good news to share with you." The bird dipped.

"Just a minute, honey."

Eacobacci tapped his finger on the casing on the telephone's mouthpiece as he waited impatiently. The bird rose, then bobbed.

"I'm back. What's the good news?"

"Bingo," said the psychologist, and his wife on the other end of the telephone line knew that her husband had hit paydirt, and found the dreamed of patient that would make him famous and them even more rich.

The bird dipped.

Chapter Two

August 1952, Bowery, New York City

I t was a disappointment. He had expected something more substantial from the building that housed the "Voice of the Jewish People".

Doctor Eacobacci stood on the broad, cracked, and mostly unclean sidewalk and looked up, a wan smile revealing his disapproval. He hoped he wasn't overdressed. He was wearing a blue, Brooks Brothers suit. No sunglasses; the sun was mostly obscured by big, gray, harmless clouds.

It was mid-morning but already hot. The traffic behind him that had already swallowed up his taxi was light and, despite his preconception of what he would find on the sidewalks of the Bowery, he stumbled over no drunken bums slumped against doorways or curled into a fetal ball anywhere in his sight, he saw no prostitutes leaning against lampposts, or men urinating on the walls of alleys. Nor did the psychologist hear the low moan of saxophones and the syncopated beat of drums wailing from the notorious bars that dotted either side of the street.

None of the four stores that were 77-79 Bowery in front of him bore even a hint of the architectural detail that Eacobacci found esthetically

He had expected something more.

interesting. It was simply a rectangular, red brick box without character, taller than it was wide, a set of three arched windows on each of the top three floors. Two-thirds of the first floor of the building was tenanted by *Annabel's Jewelry Exchange*—a shop entered through a glass door recessed between two large, plate glass windows displaying assorted, inexpensive, watches, bracelets, and trays of rings and necklaces. Since he knew nothing of the history of Gotham's oldest and longest thoroughfare, he couldn't even know if this was the original facade, or if those artistic embellishments that he so enjoyed on other buildings in Manhattan but could not even name had once existed and been subsequently removed. He made a mental note that he needed to learn more about the Big Apple's skid row.

The remaining third of the first floor was a glass door with a hand-lettered sign painted on it that he could not read in Hebrew. It meant *Tog Morgan Zhurnal.* Below that in smaller letters, and in English, was painted "The Morning Journal". Eacobacci shrugged his shoulders, walked to the smaller door, pushed it open, and entered.

Immediately, he found himself facing a long, scuffed desk and a neatly but modestly dressed young woman sitting behind the desk. She sat underneath a sign perpendicular to the wall next to her that read "Classifieds". On the desk before her was a large, gummed pad of blank forms, a cluster of yellow pencils in a can, and one black and one brown telephone.

"Good morning," she said with a smile that was more perfunctory than authentic. "May I help you?" Her teeth were slightly misaligned.

Behind her, three young women trying to look fashionable on meager salaries, sat at Spartan desks and typed at typewriters and did not look up.

"Yes, thank you. My name is Dr. Joey Eacobacci, and I'm here to talk to one of your reporters. I believe his name is Mr. Leo Rosenbaum?"

"Do you have an appointment?"

"Yes"

"Just a moment, please."

The young woman picked up the handset of the brown phone and dialed a single number. Eacobbaci realized it must be an intercom. She spoke his name into the mouthpiece; there was a pause as she listened, then she replaced the handset in its cradle.

She pointed to her left side. "Take that door down there on your left, go up the stairs, and he's the third door on the right side of the hall."

"Thank you."

The hallway at the top of the stairs was completely devoid of any sort of decoration except for small, metal signs above each of the doors that also stood perpendicular to the wall. The sign above the first door that he passed read "Managing Editor", above the second, "City Editor", and over the room he sought, "Bullpen".

The psychologist entered the bullpen and was met with six ancient scuffed desks in two parallel rows of three desks each, typewriters on each desk, and five nondescript men, four of them in shirtsleeves without ties. The fifth and furthest away from Eacobacci wore a dapper, three piece, flannel suit. The long room was also bare except for the front pages of newspapers simply thumb tacked to the walls and a calendar or two. It was otherwise filled with paper of all sorts—newspapers stacked on the floor, papers in trays, rows of filing cabinets obviously filled with paper. The sound of clacking typewriters reminded him of clusters of firecrackers exploding randomly and at a distance. In a word, the men and the room looked seedy. Every desk had overflowing ashtrays, and every face wore stubby cigarettes except for the man in the suit. He was chewing an unlit pipe.

Eacobacci stopped at the first desk and said, "Mr. Leo Rosenbaum?"

The reporter who wore a visor instead of a hat pointed his right thumb to his right without looking up at the psychologist or even raising his head.

Leo Rosenbaum raised his head to find the source of the question and stopped typing. He looked unimpressed by what he saw. He waved the doctor forward with his left hand.

"Dr. Eacobacci? How can I help you, sir?"

Eacobacci followed the invitation of the hand to the reporter's desk.

"I'm doctor Joseph Eacobacci. We talked briefly on the phone. If I may, I wanted to talk to you for a moment in more detail about your recent article on the female vigilante you newspaper people are calling 'Snake'."

"On this character, you maybe have some information?" asked the reporter.

"Possibly."

"I've got just the place where we can hear ourselves think and with a little privacy, Doctor Eacobacci. Please...?" Rosenbaum runked his chair back from the desk and pointed with his right thumb at a closed door to a small room to his right in the back wall of the bullpen.

"Your name sounds vaguely familiar to me, Doctor. We have met, maybe?" asked Rosenbaum while he opened the door to the closet that acted as the newspaper's conference room.

"Not directly."

The reporter pulled a chair back from a small table in the middle of an otherwise empty room, and waved an invitation for the doctor to sit opposite him. Eacobacci knew that every detail of his person was being studied and categorized by Rosenbaum, so he sat and returned the scrutiny.

He noted that Leo Rosenbaum was a slight man with narrow shoulders and neatly parted and groomed hair whose wire-rimmed glasses did nothing to make a nondescript face interesting. His pipe seldom left that face. He surmised that he was probably Jewish from the reporter's name and his not unpleasant physical appearance. His long face reminded the psychologist a lot of Groucho Marx without the comedian's fake mustache. Rosenbaum wore a conservative tie with broad, diagonal stripes and a stoic smile that spoke of resignation and world-weariness. Everything about him suggested reservation, caution, and a skeptical, educated, organized mind.

"I am a psychologist," began Eacobacci, "with some ties to New York City. I graduated from Columbia before getting my doctorate from Harvard."

"From New York University, I graduated," said Rosenbaum and unplugged his pipe from his face. "Please forgive my interruptions, doctor, but I'm on a deadline and a bit short of time. You said you wanted to discuss this nutty vigilante who's been robbing crooks for the last six months or so?"

"Precisely. Nutty. I've been a student of ...nutty...for most of my life, Mr. Rosenbaum, and find myself intrigued by this woman. I've read your two or three articles on her over the past few months, and thought I'd see if there wasn't something incongruous about her in one of your stories."

"Like what incongruous, Doctor?"

"In your latest story, you reported that Snake used an ax on one of her victims. All of the other accounts I've read in your newspaper and other papers haven't mentioned this kind of elevated violence. Beatings, yes. Even an account of darts being used to temporarily paralyze a thief. But, an ax?"

Rosenbaum runked his chair back from the table and stood up. There was a hint of anger on his face. He shoved his hands in his pant's pockets and began to slowly pace back and forth.

"A good eye you have, Doctor," said the reporter, and took his pipe out of his mouth. "No one has been on hand at one of her oddball robberies yet, so we don't have a single photograph of Snake. I can't even figure out how she knows to arrive when these robberies are in progress. Even the police seldom do that. Despite the popular conception that our policemen protect and serve, ninety-nine times out of a hundred they serve by mopping up *after* a crime.

"So our editorial cartoonist drew up that piece from the description given by one of the thugs who was picked up by the police soon after Snake had left the scene. That cartoonist took...shall we say...'artistic license' to illustrate the brutality used by this nutcake of a woman. There was no ax."

"Ah. I suspected as much. Do you have any additional information about this Snake character or even any speculations that you might share?"

"No info, doctor. She's an enigma wrapped in a puzzle and hidden in an onion. But you might find interesting a couple of speculations."

The reporter stopped pacing to look squarely at Eacobacci. "Speculation number one. I'm guessing that if I can break the full story about this lunatic, I'll end up on the staff of the New York Times making a living wage instead making peanuts at this penny-ante rag. And that I want very badly. I'm also guessing that you have some other motive than a passing curiosity that you aren't telling me."

"Mine is a bit stronger than a reporter's passing curiosity, Mr. Rosenbaum. That's true. About four months ago, my daughter was kidnapped. The police didn't get anywhere in finding her, and my wife and I had almost lost all hope for her recovery... alive. It was Snake who found her, freed her from her kidnappers, turned them in to the police, and brought her home to us. It made all of the newspapers."

Rosenbaum pounded his right fist into the palm of his left hand.

"I knew I'd heard your name before!"

"Considering her track record as a criminal stealing from other criminals, Mr. Rosenbaum, that made no sense. I don't do well with things that make no sense. But my wife and I still felt a very deep sense of gratitude, of course, and a very strong need to somehow thank her for saving our daughter's life."

"Leo. Please call me Leo. No one knows the first thing about this dame," said Rosenbaum. "So, on finding her, do you have a plan?"

"I don't plan on finding her," said the psychologist. "I already have."

Although he didn't do it, the reporter seemed to stagger back.

"How in Hades....?"

"We put the word out through the press and radio that we wanted to thank her personally, and she found me."

The reporter plopped down in his chair behind his desk, stunned. He took his pipe out of his face and laid it on the table.

"This is the story of the century, doctor. When did she find you? Are you knowing where she is?" he said, leaning across the desk.

"I have no idea. I was taken to her blindfolded by a black man who looked like a bum in a cab. I couldn't even see the cabbie's face. The blindfold wasn't removed until I was in a room without windows. When she was done with me, I was blindfolded and taken back to the sidewalk in front of my office in Manhattan, and pushed out of the cab."

"Did you get the medallion number of the cab?"

"No. I didn't think to look."

"The name of the cab company?"

The psychologist shook his head to indicate no.

"You said she released you when she was done with you. So, Mr. Eacobacci, for what did she want with you?"

"She accepted my thanks."

"So where you went, you don't know. So what taxi you went in, you don't know. So a detective you aren't. So go figure. Could you tell how long you were in the cab? What direction it was headed? Do you know where I can find the colored man or anything else, doctor?"

"Yes. I can tell you the one thing that I do know, that I'm not the least bit certain that this woman is 'crazy', Mr. Rosenbaum, although I do have some theories about her mental health.

"And that the black man called himself The Admiral."

"Call me crazy, Doctor Eacobacci, but it seems that you and I didn't know from peanuts when you came in here today, and you and I won't know from peanuts when you leave. Except maybe one thing.

"You and I are sitting on a powder keg.

"Or the story of the century.

"Or maybe both."

They meant nothing to Carlos Valentine, the primary muscle for the Bowery's notorious DeSalvio crime family, as he stood nervously beneath them.

The domino line of signage above him that diminished and then disappeared into the horizon advertising flophouses, store fixture outlets, bars, tattoo parlors, pawn shops, and fleabag restaurants was so familiar to the thug that they were beneath his contempt—they only bred indifference. Except for the *United States Hotel: Rooms* sign just a few yards away—he had spent sleepless nights as a young sot sweating there years earlier before he'd been saved from the life of a drunk and recruited by the founder and head of the DeSalvio crime family himself, old John DeSalvio. So also were the random zig-zags of metallic fire escapes interspersed between the signs that hung like blemishes and disfigured the facades of the two, three, four and five story brick buildings that lined both sides of Bowery Street.

Carlos twisted the *Lucky Strike* cigarette in his mouth and shoved his gnarled left hand into the pants pocket of his meticulously pressed, pin-striped suit as he stood in front of *Sammy's Bowery Follies* at 267 Bowery that occupied the ground floor of a five story brick shoebox—much longer than it was wide—next door to DeSalvio's headquarters. He swore under his breath when he found that pocket empty. A page torn from a newspaper and dancing on the broad sidewalk wrapped itself around his left foot. He frowned and kicked it free to join the other garbage on the sidewalk discarded by the bums, prostitutes, con men, artist and writers, and wide-eyed tourists that littered the Bowery.

Carlos glanced at the neon sign for *Geo Ehret's Extra Beer* hanging inside and against *Sammy's* large plate glass window, made a mental note that that's what he'd be drinking in a New York minute, then up at the large metal sign hanging perpendicular to the bar that promised patrons they'd find the "Gay 90s" inside. He had no idea what the phrase meant. The thug looked unintentionally down at two, round *7-up* logos on both of the lower corners of that window, and removed his hand from his pocket. He took the cigarette plugged into the left corner of his mouth out with his right, beefy hand, and spat.

He punched the cigarette back into his mouth, and pushed open the right of two glass doors to the immediate left of the plate glass window.

Carlos was instantly met with the smell of human sweat and urine, beer, cigarette and cigar smoke, and cheap perfumes and colognes, and with the cacophony of clinking glasses, scraping chairs, and low but chaotic human chatter that are the stuff of every bar. A neon sign for *Ruppert Beer* and rows of florescent lighting hung from the stamped tin ceiling. Most of the dingy walls were hung with a confusion of plaques, framed newspaper clippings of sporting events, and photographs.

One of the bartenders named Ham took inventory of Carlos, and, recognizing, his bulky frame, his close-set eyes, his cauliflowered left ear, and his slicked back, black hair went back to reaming out a just washed shot glass. After all, what did he care? In his boxing days, he'd fought a million of them just like Carlos.

Everyone but three of DeSalvio's men already seated at a table in the back of the bar next to a small stage hated and feared Carlos. But everyone, including his own thugs, just called him by his last name, Valentine.

It was too early for the alcoholics and tourists that usually crammed the place, so Carlos quickly reached the table always reserved for the DeSalvio crime family even when the dive was crammed with tourists out slumming, pulled out a chair unceremoniously, and plopped down like a sack of flour.

He said, "Gentlemen," without looking at any of the three. He liked to call his three subordinates gentlemen, and each responded with the nod of a head or a raised, half-empty glass of beer.

Valentine raised his arm, and a waiter appeared like magic.

"Ehret's," he said without inflection. Then watching the waiter as he made his way to the long bar opposite their table instead of at his associates, he said to his cronies, "What's the word on the street?"

"Nothin' much, boss," Danny Costello answered, and lifted his mug for a swig.

"Good. Good. That means that the above-grounds has gotten th' message I sent by way of th' below-grounds and I'm doin' my job. What's on the schedule?"

"Nothin' big," said Chuck Ferrara, the second of Valentine's associates. Vinnie's runnin' th' numbers, Martie's takin' care of th' ladies, and the Miller boys are goin' to make a withdrawal from the bank of Friday. Everything's smooth."

The waiter appeared magically at Valentine's side, and a cold mug appeared in Carlos' hand. He removed his cigarette from his mouth, laid it on the edge of the half-filled ash tray in the middle of the table covered with a dingy, checkerboard table cloth, and took a long sip. "Now, let's talk about th' schedule fer next week."

The tug on the calf of his left pants leg caught Valentine by surprise.

"Hey!" he barked, and looked down.

He looked down into the mutilated face of a train wreak, a middle-aged stumble-bum who couldn't stumble anymore because his legs had been blown off in North Korea. The left side of his sallow face had been crushed and poorly repaired, his left eye was larger than his right eye, and his dirty, stringy hair hung from beneath a nautical cap to his shoulders. Jack Flash sat on a square of plywood propelled on little wheels taken from the feet of an office chair, and the derelict held a paddle with half of its haft missing across his chest with both hands as he grinned up at Valentine with a picket fence of mostly missing teeth.

He said, "Bumblefunny."

Jack had also lost half of his mind during America's latest police action.

"Get lost, ya cripple; I'm busy here," Valentine growled, and turned back to his associates. "As I was sayin', let's talk about our dance card fer next week."

The second tug on the calf of his left pant's leg left Valentine irritated.

"I said get lost," said the thug without looking at the cripple, "and the next time I have to say it, Jack, I'll bash yer head in."

The double amputee said, "Fardle," and opened the hole in the lower third of his stubbled face some called a mouth and pointed at it with the dirty, index finger of his dirty right hand. He added, "beer".

Valentine half-rose from his chair, his face distorted with anger. It was Danny's hand on his forearm that restrained him from rising to his full height.

"Ignore him, boss," Danny said, "He's just a harmless half-wit."

Valentine said, "Shut up, Danny. You think you're tellin' me something I don't already know?" and then sat down heavily. He added, "Ok, bud, you asked for it."

Then he picked up his mug and slowly poured his beer in Jack's up-turned face. Jack sputtered and gasped as he initially tried to catch as much of the beer as possible in his mouth. But there was too much of it, and the cripple began to choke. Valentine laughed and his associates joined him in his laughter as Jack Flash continued to gag.

"Had enough?" asked Carlos when the beer mug was empty. "Army boy."

He then placed his left foot with its polished $100 shoe on the edge of Jack's plywood platform, and shoved it hard.

The platform and Jack careened backwards toward the long bar. He lost the paddle he used to propel himself as he skidded across the sawdust covered floor, striking the leg of a customer of *Sammy's* who yelped in pain, only to ricochet off him and hit an unoccupied chair at the second unoccupied table closest to Valentine that stopped him.

Jack fell off of his platform with a heavy thud and lay on the floor. His cap fell off of his long, brown, nasty hair matted with beer, and he began blubbering, his eyes welling with tears and the stubs of what had once been his legs began flailing in the air.

The double amputee blubbered, "I'll kill you," making one of the biggest mistakes of his life. Valentine heard him.

Eyes in the bar began to turn to find the source of the noise as Valentine runked his chair back, rose, and followed the recent path of the crippled veteran. His three subordinate thugs rose to stand at their table. When he reached Jack, Valentine bent at the waist, raised his left arm high above his shoulder, and backhand slapped Jack.

Jack Flash grunted. One of the three bartenders reached for a telephone as the second of the three bartenders fled for the front door. Ham, who had made his call earlier, watched the event unfolding with a wary eye.

"I told you what I'd do," said Valentine. "And I'm a man of my word."

Valentine raised his right arm high above his shoulder, and slapped Jack again.

As Jack Flash moaned on the floor, holding both sides of his head with his dirty hands, Valentine swung his right leg back and high, and kicked the bum in the ribs.

"I said," he barked with grim fury, "get away."

He kicked the cripple in the left arm as Jack gasped and rolled from side to side, clutching his ribs. "Maybe now you'll know I mean what I say."

Customers were rising from tables and heading for the entrance to *Sammy's* when the voice said:

"F. D. R. said," she hissed with a voice like a snake, "'we have nothing to fear but fear itself'. I agree."

Every eye left in the bar followed the voice to the stage.

The Kabuki mask she wore did not look happy.

Snake stood there, her hands on her hips, wearing her dark blue bustier with leather flames, leather armlets, black tights, and high, stiletto boots that rose just above her calves. In her left hand, she held a quarterstaff easily five feet long topped by a bronze snake's head. Her blacksnake whip was coiled on her left hip.

Her long, brown hair fell like satin to the top of her bustier. She threw back and shook her hair and laughed like a man, then said:

"It is fun to be in the same decade with you! Look out boys, it's time to party!"

All Hell broke loose in the space of five seconds.

Valentine and his three goons standing at their table all reached into their suits and pulled out guns. A woman somewhere in the bar screamed. Chairs were overturned as the few who'd remained in the bar changed their minds. The bartender holding the telephone cupped his hand around the mouthpiece as he spoke. The remaining bartender, named Ham, watched Valentine, Snake, and Jack as if watching for an opportunity to join the coming fray.

Danny Costello fired his weapon and missed the woman in leather who, pivoting towards him, pointed her right arm at the goon, and pressed two fingers into the palm of her hand. There was a tiny *thwip* sound and Danny fell face forward onto the table, a dart jutting from his neck. The two remaining DeSalvio thugs pushed Danny off of the table, turned it over, and squatted behind it in an attempt to use it as a shield.

"It's alive, it's alive!" Snake shouted, and once again throwing her head back and shaking her cascading mane of hair, laughed hysterically.

Before a second gun shot could be squeezed off, Snake vaulted off of the stage using her quarterstaff as a pole. Her body almost completely horizontal, her two rigid legs struck the top of the table like a pile-driver, knocking it and DeSalvio's men back hard against the wall behind them and scattering the chairs like kindling.

Valentine watched, stunned, as she twirled her quarterstaff like a baton and then struck the guns, one at a time, out of the hands of each of his remaining goons.

She said, "When you reach the end of your rope..." and struck one of the two thugs a glancing blow with the quarterstaff on the left side of his temple..."Tie a knot in it and hang on." The thug fell like an ox.

She said, "Above all, try something," and struck the last thug a crushing blow with her quarterstaff on the right side of his temple. He and his gun fell like a wet sack of flour to the floor.

The last customer in *Sammy's Bowery Follies* disappeared through the front door.

Then Valentine was on her. Grabbing her right shoulder from behind, he spun her around and punched her hard in the face with all of his strength.

Her Kabuki mask cracked and was pushed askance, blocking her vision, as she stumbled back and back and back and hit the wall behind her with crushing force. She slumped to the floor.

"Crazy bitch," snarled Valentine, and leveled his gun, and fired.

Her right shoulder jerked back, and Snake looked down to watch blood fill the rip in her leather costume high up on her bicep.

Valentine was on her again. He jerked Snake up off of the floor by her neck, her face only inches from his, and snarled, "You ain't worth a goddamn bullet, sister. I'm going to beat you to death and enjoy every minute of it."

Her voice muffled by her askew Kabuki mask, and her quarterstaff lying on the floor where she had dropped it, Snake gasped, "Let us move forward...with strong and active...faith."

Then she head-butted Valentine.

The thug staggered back several feet, clutching his forehead with his left hand, his gun forgotten in his right fist. In one, graceful, continuous motion, Snake stepped quickly back, straightening her Kabuki mask as she did so that she could see, snatched her blacksnake whip off of her hip, dropped its popper to lay its length on the floor, then jerked it up high.

She said, "Be sincere, be brief, be seated."

The whip's thong lashed out, wrapped around his face, and the popper bit the unprotected flesh of Valentine's cheek.

He howled and dropped his gun, clutching the blacksnake whip's thong still coiled around his face. There was red oozing between the spaces between his fingers.

Grasping its butt in both hands, Snake jerked her whip back.

Jolted forward, Valentine stumbled into a table and chairs, and all crashed in a jumble of wood and bruised flesh to the floor.

His gun skidded across the floor and out of his grip.

Like an angel of death, Snake was at the thug's side in four determined strides.

She dropped her blacksnake whip, raised her left arm high above her shoulder, and backhand slapped Valentine across his bleeding face where he lay. He grunted.

She raised her right arm high above her shoulder, and slapped Valentine again.

She clutched the bleeding slash in her right arm with her left hand and said, "Ouch. It's not the size of the dog in the fight; it's the fight in the dog."

As DeSalvio's muscle man moaned on the floor, clutching both sides of his face with his hands, Snake swung her right leg back and high, and kicked him in the ribs.

"What comes around, tough guy, goes around," she snarled.

She kicked him in the left arm and he rolled away from her, clutching his ribs.

"That's for the cripple," she added.

Almost within reach of them, Jack Flash giggled and clapped his hands.

She said, "I pledge you, I pledge myself, to a New Deal for the American People,"

then stood silently for a long moment to watch for movement. There was none.

She removed a fan of cards stamped with a striking cobra and let them fall like drops of blood on Valentine's body.

Snake picked up her whip from the jumble of wood and Valentine on the floor. She said, "Hold your applause, please," to the almost empty bar. She turned and walked back to where her quarterstaff lay on the floor, and picked it up with her right hand.

She looked at her wounded right bicep again.

She said, "I tought I thaw a puddy tat."

Then Snake walked with unhurried and sure steps to Jack Flash and knelt by his side. With some effort, she got him back upright on his plywood square, and placed an arm around his shoulders to steady him there. Then she pulled the strands of dirty hair that covered his left ear back and whispered, "This generation of Americans has a rendezvous with destiny. Hello, lover. Welcome home."

The remaining barkeeps behind the bar and close to the stage applauded as Snake carefully rolled Jack Flash to the back door of *Sammy's*. Ham added a wink.

He couldn't see through her cracked Kabuki mask, but Ham knew she had returned his wink.

He said, mostly to himself, "Hurrah for yourself, baby, but 'The Hammer' ain't gonna like this one bit."

Ten minutes later, the police arrived.

Chapter Three

Berlin, Nov., 1944, Geheimstaafpolizel (Gestapo) Headquarters

"**T**hey have been murdering the leaders of our Holy Reich, killing us like flies," said Colonel Wolfgang Pfingste as he shoved his chair back from his oversized desk and rose to his feet. "We are the Master Race, and these murdering Jewish rat-pigs and their Russian lapdogs must and will be stopped!"

Wolfgang began to pace back and forth behind his massive desk with his pudgy hands clutched behind his back. They were weak, uncalloused hands that had never known hard labor. The stunning, blonde movie starlet who was poured into the chair across from his desk and wore a powder blue dress that accented her sexuality said nothing and showed no emotional response to his desperate, heated diatribe.

The words that Greta Hoffmeyer said inside her head, however, included *pompous jackass, strutting peacock* and *stupid fool*.

It was not the first time she'd thought those phrases. The words came often and easily for a woman with long, blonde hair that swept to her shoulders, large, deep blue, penetrating eyes, high cheek bones, flawless almond skin, full lips, a heart-shaped jaw, and a body that made men ache.

Before Colonel Wolfgang had begun to rant, she had already taken in and memorized all of the details of the small, austere room that they were in, one of many that served the immediate needs of the grand destiny of the Nazis' counter-espionage agency, Brillensschlange, or "Cobra", in which she had served with dedication and excellence as its most effective female operative. Greta's visual inventory had found no threats in the room to Wolfgang's or her security. She trusted no one, and it was a standard procedure for her. It was, after all, an important part of her job.

She also noted that there were no longer framed paintings or tapestries stolen from the Jewish or French or Polish people in France, or Poland, or Austria hanging on his walls, or flowers on his desk next to the small, red flag that, furled, still did not obscure its swastika. She noticed a half-folded newspaper laying next to the flag. Nor did the frayed cuffs of Wolfgang's wrinkled uniform or his untrimmed hair pass her notice. The Colonel's scuffed boots were no longer shined. It was to be expected. After all, all supplies, including luxuries like food and bullets, were daily growing more and more scarce. The severe shortages were even beginning to affect the citizens of Berlin, now eerily silent between the savage howls of the scattered and infrequent bombings; many would gladly slaughter and eat a horse if they could find one. It was so because the **God-Men** of Germany were losing their war to conquer the inferior races of the world and they knew it, although it was never spoken aloud.

She knew that he knew that she knew what could not be spoken. Hitler had eyes and ears everywhere, even spies spying on spies. Deception and denial had become all pervasive in the Fatherland.

Greta's powers of observation, a natural gift honed to perfection beginning with her initial service in the *Hitler Youth League of German Worker Youth,* was only one of the reasons she was Germany's top female spy. So she patiently sat and watched as her superior officer strutted and fretted. His heightened emotional performance was certainly no surprise. Her most important gift was that she knew men.

"As you well know," continued Colonel Pfingste, "it is these secret resistance groups that have been killing us off, Fraulein Hoffmeyer. As you know, one headed by Colonel Henning Von Treschow and General Friedrich Olbricht is already credited with a failed attempt to assassinate our Fuehrer on July 20th. Traitors and fools, every one."

"Yes," she said, "How could you think that I wouldn't know?"

"Of course, of course, of course," he blubbered, somewhat embarrassed.

"Don't be embarrassed," she said. "It usually takes more than three weeks to prepare a good impromptu speech'. That's Mark Twain."

"What?" he asked, stopping in mid-step.

"Go on, go on," she encouraged the strutting peacock with a dismissive wave of her hand.

His words began to blur and fade into an indistinguishable mumbling as she continued to assess her immediate 'superior'—a middle-aged, pudgy, married man with close-set eyes and of less than average height and intelligence, with slicked-back black hair and the shadow of stubble on his pallid chin and cheeks—the very antithesis of Hitler's Aryan **God-Man**, as were most of the Nazis, and as was Hitler himself. Deception of the masses and self-deception had been the Nazis' stock and trade for long, weary years now. Aünd Gretchen had no illusions about it or regrets about her own participation in the great lie.

She had learned that life was a lie in the worst possible of ways. Men were a lie. And Greta knew men better than they knew themselves, better than the back of her own hand—a hand that had been so useful in manipulating the simple, hedonistic animals. They were all of the same cut with only slight variations in their obsessions, the primary one being lust. The loud-mouthed, overbearing, domineering ones were the easiest to use, hiding their inadequacies and fears behind a facade of superiority and power. The quiet ones weren't much more complicated. Men all wanted pampering, attention, adoration, even worship. They all hungered for power, superiority—indeed, to be feared. They all craved sex with as many women as possible without consequence or commitment, and to be told that they were the best lover in the world. And they all wanted their women to be submissive, under their thumbs.

Men were all drooling fools...and so useful.

"Fraulein Hoffmeyer, are you listening?"

"Oh course, of course, Colonel," she lied as she snapped out of her reverie. "Please remind me, dear. Why did you request this meeting today?"

"Now a group called '*Sieg*' threatens our Fuehrer," Pfingste began again as he eyed Greta suspiciously, "and we believe that a plastic surgeon, Dr. Maxwell Riegelmann, is a member of these traitors and fanatics who call themselves 'Victory'."

Pfingste plopped down in his chair, opened the newspaper to its full length, and pushed it across the desk in front of Greta. She looked at a classified section that was greatly abbreviated because of the war; the Colonel had circled one of the "Help Wanted" advertisements in red pencil.

"What is this?" she asked, leaning partially across the desk and picking up Pfingste's newspaper. "Are they still printing newspapers?"

"Read the one circled," said Wolfgang. The tone of his voice spoke of a rapid loss of interest. He was somewhat spent after his amazing performance.

"Fraulein Hoffmeyer, are you listening?"

Greta read "Wanted, experienced receptionist for medical office." The name of Dr. Max Riegelmann followed a description of the receptionist's responsibilities with the address of his office in Berlin.

"Your assignment," said Colonel Wolfgang, "requiring your immediate and entire attention, one at which you must not—no—cannot fail, is to save the *Führer*!"

"As a receptionist in a medical office," Greta said and folded the newspaper, laid it back down on Wolfgang's desk, and pushed it back to her superior officer. "Being a spy certainly isn't as glamorous as they portray it in the movies.

"Such a strong statement, Colonel," she continued, checking the condition of her fingernail polish on her right hand. "Must. No. Cannot. Are you questioning my loyalty to Adolph or the effectiveness of my service to the *Führer*? Can you name one other person whose intelligence has left a greater swath of death on the battlefield or sent more of 'God's Chosen Ones' to concentration camps?"

"No, no, no, Fraulein Hoffmeyer. You are here, in this room, now, because I have no greater confidence in anyone than in you!"

As she stood up and smoothed the wrinkles from her dress, Greta said, "Ah. Well, then, you know you have nothing to fear. The *Führer* is saved."

As Greta walked away from his desk, Pfingste watched her with the thrill and disgust, the excitement and repulsion, the purity of the Super Man and the rutting hunger of The Beast for sex, that were at war in every man, even in men like him who loved their wives. He also knew two things with absolute certainty. One of Hitler's greatest assets, proven unlike the *Führer*'s ridiculous gigantic orbiting solar mirrors, or his flying discord aircraft, fireballs, or super bombs, was completely under his thumb.

And that another rat-pig, Max Riegelmann, was as good as dead.

The rain that fell from the same, gray, overcast sky now rained Allied bombs and death at random, at unexpected times on the dark streets of Berlin.

The rain fell on damaged and broken pavement where only the depraved, destitute, and desperate citizens of the once magnificent city walked now. As it drizzled, it dripped down the black umbrella that Dr. Max Riegelmann held over his head with a hand that shook slightly because of the secret he carried. It dripped down the brim of his soaked Fedora to wet his slicker as he stood at the foot of the stoop of an indigent, three story tenement building in the ghetto.

The pitter-patter of falling rain was the only sound that night on the otherwise silent street where the little Jewish doctor stood.

Max was thirty-two years old with streaks of gray at his temples, an ugly birthmark on his left cheek, a face pockmarked from acne, and slightly hunchbacked. He shifted his weight from his left leg to his right as he fidgeted in the malformed body of a near-dwarf in which he had never felt at ease. He was only four-feet-seven inches tall, Jewish, and ranked as among the most brilliant medical doctors in Germany. That he was a brilliant surgeon was why he was Jewish *and* still alive. The Nazis turned their heads as well as stuck their noses in the air when their need outweighed their racism.

Shifting his weight from his left to his right foot in indecision was nothing new for Max. He had spent his life standing outside of dances that didn't allow freaks to dance, outside of rooms where clubs met that excluded people who did not look like them, outside of lichés in High School and University, outside of parties, and sports teams, and had never experienced a stolen moment of fulfilled adolescent passion.

Outside and desperately alone.

The Nazis were not the only ones who turned their heads, looked away, and stuck their noses up in the air when Max was near.

Indeed, life would have been intolerable without his fraternal twin brother, Franz

Max finally screwed up his courage, furtively glanced a final time to his left and then his right side, ascended the steps, and entered the building even when to do so might mean certain torture or death if even a single Nazi eye were on him.

The silence in the shoddy tenement hallway lit by a single, naked light bulb hanging from the ceiling was broken only by the sound of his soggy footsteps as he moved quickly and with certainty to the third doorway on his left. Max stopped, put his hand on the doorknob, tested it, opened the door gingerly, slowly, and stepped through onto the top landing of a short flight of stairs. He closed the door behind him.

Riegelmann heard faint, clandestine whispers rise from the dimly lit room below as he began to descend the stairs, lowering and then folding up his umbrella as he did so. The whispers became voices that grew louder as he descended until someone heard his footsteps. The voices fell silent.

Six rigid, anxious men seated in rickety, wooden folding chairs in a semi-circle in the center of the small room, watched Max reach the foot of the stairs. None of them had ever lived in a ghetto or even visited one until recently, the majority were not Jewish, and all wore the dead expression of men under intense pressure. One man tall, and straight, and still speaking, was the focus of the semi-circle until they heard the intruder.

All of them watched Max. Three of the men seated who had never held a gun until a few months ago, held pistols pointed at his chest. The man standing smiled. He interrupted his speech and said: "Maxwell! Come in! Sit! You are late!"

The man standing was Franz, first born of the fraternal Riegelmann twins and therefore also thirty-two years old. But there were no streaks of gray at his temples, no ugly birthmark, no face pockmarked from acme, and no hump on his back. Fritz was blond and handsome, with the muscular body of a near-Adonis in which he had always felt at home. He was six-feet-three inches tall, Jewish, and was ranked high among Adolf's elite Schutzstaffell (SS) troops. Indeed, he was one of Hitler's most trusted personal bodyguards *because* he looked exactly like the *Führer*'s image of a perfect blonde and blue-eyed Aryan and nothing like Max.

It was a great secret but no surprise that his last name had been falsified, changed to Schroeder. He had changed his surname because no one who was not an Aryan—no Jew—could be considered a German citizen, much less serve in Germany's military. He had joined the SS to save his life—the life, by his own admission, of a coward.

Initially, the greater surprise had been that he and Max were Jewish.

As the children of fourth generation Hebrew immigrants, they had been raised as Germans and always thought of themselves as Germans. They had known almost nothing of Jewish culture or of Judaism. Then Hitler had passed the Nuremberg Laws in 1933 that defined what constituted being an "Aryan" and they had become Jewish.

Hitler had determined that anyone with one Jewish parent (one half-blood) was considered a Jew. Those with one Jewish grandparent (one fourth-blood) were Germans unless they "looked Jewish". In addition, the Nazis considered the shape of the skull to be of paramount importance in looking Jewish. Therefore, Max had the wrong shape under his hat and was Jewish; Franz did not and could and did pass as Aryan.

Max took his hat off of his Jewish head and held it at his side in his left hand as he began to unbutton his slicker with his right hand. One of the seated men with a cigarette dangling from his mouth stood up, moved to a folded chair leaning against a wall, and unfolded it. He returned to the semi-circle of men as two of them made room for the additional chair. Max tossed his Fedora on the chair.

"I'm sorry I'm late," Max said as he picked his hat up off of the chair and sat down. "I was unavoidably detained by a patient, the whore of a Nazi officer."

"...our boot is on the neck of the snake," Franz continued, ignoring Max's remark. "And soon, so very soon, we will crush the head of Cobra, of the Schutzstaffell, of the Gestapo, and of the false head of the mockery of our nation created by that snake, Adolf Hitler. We are on the verge of Victory because of my strategic but incomplete knowledge of his movements and habits, and because of the financial support gathered by my brother, Max. We will succeed, and soon; we will taste the victory denied to so many of our brothers."

"It's amazing what a Nazi will say under the influence of the right anesthetic," said Max without false modesty to the man sitting next to him. "The raising of the money, easy." Franz overheard his brother, grinned, and continued his speech.

"You know that I am no hero. I have kept no secrets. I have confessed my sins. You know that I stand before you with innocent blood on my hands. But I swear to you that I will wash that blood away with the blood of a madman or will die trying.

"Each of our escape routes is in place. If we succeed but must flee, we will return someday and greet one another as brothers. If I fail and you are discovered, you must not hesitate to take flight from our Fatherland, possibly for the rest of your lives.

"I'm done. That's all I had to say. Remember, everyone of us must keep every word spoken at our *Sieg* meetings secret. To do otherwise is certain death. Keep me in your prayers. Go home knowing that if we never meet again that we did not meet in vain. From my lips to God's ears."

The seated men began to rise and drift into groups to talk among themselves, Franz removed a package of cigarettes from his pocket with a matchbook, removed a cigarette and stuck it in his mouth, lit it, and returned the matches and cigarettes to his shirt pocket. He inhaled a long draw of smoke as Max joined him.

"You don't have to do this," said Max. "Someone else..."

"Yes, I do have to do this, Max. It's time that I did something to make mom and dad proud of their son instead of ashamed of a traitor to our race and people."

"That's crazy talk. Our parents are dead, Franz."

"I know that as Jews we're not supposed to believe in heaven or hell, Max, but I still do. So, if the very worst happens, I'll just be stepping through a door from one life to the next. So, what's so bad about that, I ask you?"

Franz took his cigarette out of his mouth, bent down and hugged his brother. When he straightened, there may have been tears in his eyes.

"It's time for you to go home. I wish I could walk there with you, but you know that's impossible. You were last in, so why don't you leave first, little Max. And be careful. Remember, not a word about any of this to anyone. And look both ways before you cross the street, or you might get run over by a Nazi tank."

"Franz …."

"No, no, no. There is nothing left to say. Go home, Max. Go home."

Max Riegelmann's walk home was long, cold, dreary, and wet, but uneventful. But as he stood with his key in his hand before the door of his apartment, in what once had been an exclusive, rich neighborhood in Berlin, the same quote from Benjamin Franklin that he had memorized at University and that had pestered him like a gadfly during his return home continued to gnaw at Max.

It was a thought he had fought to dislodge, to erase, to shake out of his head.

He had failed. It was:

"Three can keep a secret if two of them are dead."

August 1952, Bowery, New York City

With his head thrown back, the blade of his broken paddle occasionally slapping the floor to propel him, Jack Flash spun around and around and around on his little wooden platform, laughing. Four days after his beating at *Sammy's Bowery Follies*, his shipwreck of a face was still bruised and cut, but bandaged.

Jack was laughing because he was dancing with legs in slow motion through a hail of bullets in North Korea and no bullet tore away the flesh from an arm or drilled a hole through his heart or smashed half of his head into a jelly of blood and brains, and because he had a secret.

He wasn't really Jack Flash.

His real name was Herman Jones, and he was a recently discharged American soldier through and through from Shawnee Oklahoma. And he wasn't really dancing with death in North Korea. Jack Flash was spinning like a dervish in Wonderland.

He didn't know and he didn't care that Wonderland was really an abandoned warehouse on the backside of the Bowery because his mind was shattered.

The massively muscled bartender, named Ham, who had called Snake on the telephone the moment that Carlos Valentine had opened the front door of *Sammy's* four nights ago sat in on a metal folding chair and watched Jack dance. He wasn't smiling. Around him was a wide array of gymnastic equipment including dumbbells, a leg-extension machine, treadmill, punching bag, pommel horse, parallel bars, and twenty-four ounce clubs. He had used most of it during his boxing days. Outside of throwing a bowling ball at the Four Seasons bowling alley in Jersey at something that looked like the clubs, Ham seldom used exercise equipment anymore.

Jack jammed the blade of his paddle against the floor to clumsily stop his spin. As a door opened on the far end of the warehouse, he gasped for breath, saluted, and said:

"Yes sir, Captain Spaulding!"

Snake stood in the doorway in her Kabuki mask with a cobra coiled around her left eye down her cheek to the tip of her chin and a gray sweatsuit. In her arms was a square, wooden platform with small wheels on the side facing Ham and Jack. She said:

"Hello boys, it's me, Mae," Snake said without the hissing of a snake. "I used to be Snow White, but I drifted."

"Hello, Mae," answered Ham. "Always a pleasure."

"I see ya accepted my invitation to come up and see me sometime," she said. In ten resolute steps, she had joined the two men. Neither of them were counting the steps. She laid the wooden platform on its wheels next to Jack Flash.

Someone had bolted what looked like a woman's side saddle for riding horses, but without the stirrups or cinching straps onto the top of the platform. A safety belt had been added, and a flat toggle switch on its right corner.

Snake squatted next to Jack. She smiled, gently stroked his right cheek, and said, "Glad to see you're on the mend, Jack. Hope you appreciate what I did for you at the bar."

The double amputee vigorously shook his head indicating yes.

"Good, good. Would you like to help *me* now?"

Jack vigorously shook his head indicating yes.

"If you can, you'll get three squares a day, a place to sleep, some pocket change, and a new friend. Me. What do you say?

Jack said, "Nordack."

"I take that as a yes," continued Snake. "There's no question you're nutty as a fruit cake...just like me. So the real question is can you hear, understand, and repeat what other people say around you. Like on the sidewalk or at *Sammy's* or *Al's* or any other bar. Now, if you can, repeat after me. Ten, seven, four, fifteen, two hundred and five."

Jack said, "I take that as a yes. Now, if you can, repeat after me. Ten, seven, four, fifteen, two hundred and five."

"Ah. Good, Jack Flash, good. Between two evils, I always pick the one I never tried before."

Jack repeated her words.

"Meet me at the corner of fifty-second and eighth street," said Snake, "at eight o-clock Tuesday night."

Jack repeated what Snake had said.

"Good. Good. Bring that hot twenty-two that you stole from the cop."

Jack repeated her words. Snake rose from her squatting position and gestured with her right hand for Ham to join them. He did so.

"Jack, please lay your paddle on the floor. We are going to lift you off of your little platform and place you on your new home, custom built to fit you. Ham, when you leave today, you'll throw the old one into a dumpster."

"Done and done," answered the barkeep, and helped lift a puzzled but compliant Jack off of his old platform and onto his new vehicle. Snake strapped him in as she said:

"Now you won't fall off as much, lover. And if you push this toggle..." she pushed it. "Little brakes lock your wheels in place and you can't be pushed around anymore."

When Jack looked up into her emotionless Kabuki mask, there were tears of gratitude in his red rimmed eyes.

"You are going to become one of my snitches, and a very effective one I'd say. And, today, you are going to learn how to protect yourself while you do it."

Jack Flash made a gun with his hand. "Bang, Bang? Kill th' bastards!"

"No, no gun yet, soldier boy. The first rule of my Nest of Vipers is no one is ever killed. And even a madwoman, like me, doesn't put a gun in the hand of a madman. I generally avoid temptation unless I can't resist it. But at those time when *you* can't, Jack, you will need a way to protect yourself, something not obvious to someone attacking you. The element of surprise, if you will. We are going to turn your paddle into a weapon. But before I do any physical exertion, I always warm up. Watch."

In rapid succession, she effortlessly performed a series of toe-touches, jumping jacks, arm circles, trunk rotations, and front and side lunges.

"Incredible," said the barkeep with barefaced lust. "Do you have a boy-friend, boss? Just asking."

"It is better to be looked over than overlooked," Snake quipped.

Turning back to Jack, she added: "Later, I'll design some warm up ex-ercises specially for you Jack. But for now..." Snake picked up his paddle from the floor.

Using the shaft of the paddle like a foil with its blade close to her body, Snake powerfully lunged, then parried with an imaginary opponent. Then using the paddle as a pole, she somersaulted one, two, three times to the punching bag, pounded it viciously ten times and alternately with the shaft and the blade of the paddle, and finally turned to face her audience.

Ham and Jack were immobile and slack jawed.

As she took confident, long strides across the floor of the warehouse to rejoin Jack and Ham, she riposted, fleched, and remised with the oar.

"When I'm good, I'm very good, baby. But when I'm bad, I'm better. Now, with your weapon," she said, and squatted, swinging the paddle in a vicious, wide arc, "you cut your enemy down at the knees. When he falls," she continued, rising. "You strike again, like this."

She swung the paddle over her head and then struck the floor. She swung the shaft of the paddle under her left underarm, and bowed.

"Be careful about reading health books. You may die of a misprint," she said.

Snake straightened, and both men wished they could see the hatred, seething rage, or calm, emotionless expression on her face beneath that inscrutable Kabuki mask.

She handed the broken oar to Jack Flash.

"It's a dangerous world out there," she said. "Just remember, boys. You only live once, but if you do it right, once is enough."

Chapter Four

Berlin, November, 1944 Gestapo Headquarters

Dr. Max Riegelmann swallowed very hard and wiped his sweaty hands on his medical smock. He had never seen her in one of her minor roles in a movie; he was much too busy and lacked the imagination to enjoy movies. So his nervous first impression had more to do with his complete inexperience with women entangled with the animal instinct hardwired in every man to procreate. Even in a highly educated, ugly man, consciously admitting that inexperience and animal lust did nothing to lessen their subconscious influence on every aspect of his life.

Across from his meticulously organized desk in his once plush office sat Miss Gretchen Lagle, her long, red hair cascading to perfect, gently rounded shoulders, her large, deep-blue eyes penetrating into the depths of his soul, her high, rosy cheek bones, flawless almond skin, full strawberry lips, and heart-shaped jaw all putting flesh on every man's secret fantasies.

And her body! He could not take his eyes off of her body, which made no sense. He was a doctor. He well knew all of the types of mucous and secretions and rashes and diseases that dampened lust. He had peeled skin back from ruptured blood vessels, raw muscle, and nerve, and traveled the swamp of internal organs countless times. Although Max had never had a girlfriend, he wasn't even a complete stranger to sex. He had been with a prostitute once. And yet...

Miss Gretchen Lagle held a newspaper loosely rolled up into a tube in her right hand; her left lay demurely in her lap clutching a small, almond colored purse. She wore a modest, pastel green dress with a cloth belt at the waist, and a pillbox hat. Her dress had cinched up a bit when she had sat down revealing a pair of beautiful, pink, un-stockinged calves ending in simple, black leather shoes. Although modest, that dress nevertheless did nothing but accentuate everything that made women sexually attractive to men.

Max imagined she smelled like almonds.

"Have you had time to review my resume, Dr. Riegelmann?" she said in a husky alto and crossed her legs. "I have several years experience working in an office, and I'm sure that I can do the job for you. Dr. Riegelmann?"

"What?" he asked, startled out of his reverie. "Excuse me, Miss...?"

"Gretchen. Gretchen Lagle, doctor."

Making sure that his words were not halting or that he did not stammer, Max said:

"Oh, of course, yes. The job is not complicated. It is basically answering the telephone, scheduling appointments, helping me manage my time, and coordinating surgeries with hospitals. I'm afraid it doesn't pay that much because of the war and all."

"I've done my homework, Dr. Reigelmann, and am told you are one of the finest surgeons in all of Germany. Working with you in any way would be an honor, and I would think of fulfilling my duties as a receptionist as playing a small role in a very important work...yours."

"That was a gracious thing to say, Miss Lagle..."

"Please," Gretchen interrupted. "Please call me Gretchen."

"I wish I could pay a better wage...Gretchen, but we have all had to sacrifice for the war, and my business is down."

"I am certain," smiled Gretchen, "that I will more than earn my salary, Dr. Reigelmann. And I am certain that when our glorious march to...victory...is fulfilled and we rule the world as the Master Race, I will be more than compensated. *Heil Hitler!*"

She raised her right hand in the Nazi salute.

"Yes, *Heil*," Max responded, successfully hiding his disgust from long practice. "Let me see, now. You have brought a resume?"

"Certainly," she said, and leaned across the desk making sure that she exposed as much of her breasts as possible within the limits of her modest dress.

He picked up her resume from the top of his desk and pretended to study it for some long moments.

"Your references are excellent," Max continued, peeking around the edge of the resume he held in front of him. "I will contact them today. You have both the education and experience I desire.

"I can't imagine your references not checking out, so I see no reason that I shouldn't offer you the job. If your references are acceptable, can you start Monday?"

"I think I already have, Dr. Riegelmann," said Gretchen, and winked her left eye.

The seduction began on Monday with a sideways glance and then another, and a coy smile, and titillating laughter at his failed attempts at humor, her hand gently placed on Dr. Riegelmann's forearm, and continued on Tuesday with a glimpse of her cleavage offered innocently to the doctor. Flattery at his high position in German society and with the elite of the Master Race followed, and sexual innuendo stoked the long smoldering fires on Wednesday and Thursday. But Gretchen's most seductive nuance was that she did not look away when Max entered the outer office where she pretended to work, and did not look away when their eyes met directly.

Friday's fall was quick because Max had never fallen before except in his dreams.

On the following Monday, her smiles and touches and laughter led to shared coffee before the office opened (after several days, he would bring rare pastries), then lunches followed at one of the few remaining restaurants still open in Berlin when his busy scheduled allowed (she made certain they were allowed), and finally a supper to evaluate her first week as his receptionist.

She got a raise.

For the entire dance, the word date was never mentioned, but by the eighth day, after occasional gifts for Gretchen including a book of poetry, an aromatic candle, and a modest box of chocolates, Max knew that, beyond belief or explanation, and for the first time in his horribly lonely, empty life, a real and beautiful flesh and blood woman did not find him absolutely repulsive.

His belief strengthened Gretchen's belief in self-delusion.

As their romance deepened, so deepened the war and the season of public denial and private despair, of tedious and unending fear, grief, and shame in Berlin. Everyone knew that the *Siege* of their beloved city was inevitable.

On their last Friday evening together, Max sat nervously across a small table from Gretchen who seemed more beautiful, more demure, and more desirable with each passing day.

"I have a little something for you, tonight," he said, and pushed a small, long, rectangular box across the table, lowering his eyes as he did so.

"Maxwell, dearest," Gretchen cooed as he began to open the box. "You don't need to buy my affection for you with gifts. You must stop this. I really…"

She looked down at a modestly expensive bracelet of precious stones inlaid in a low grade of gold that must have cost a fortune because of the war. She leaned across the table, placed the cool palm of her right hand against his left cheek, and placed a lingering kiss on his lips. She sat down.

Max Riegelmann was struck dumb. It was the first romantic kiss he'd ever received in his thirty two years of quite loneliness.

That night, Gretchen put Max's relatively inexpensive bauble in her jewelry box that was hidden under clothing in the top drawer of her chest of drawers in her apartment.

The little box was full of expensive jewelry given to her by men she had seduced, deceived, and betrayed.

Colonel Wolfgang Pfingste paced back and forth like a caged animal behind his massive desk with his pudgy hands clinched behind his back. Gretchen Lagle sat cool and composed in the chair across from his desk saying nothing and showing no emotional response to his desperate, angry words.

"Calm yourself, Wolfgang," said Gretchen. "It isn't the end of the world. You're going to give yourself another heart attack."

Wolfgang stopped suddenly and unexpectedly and pounded the edge of his desk with his right fist. Now, there were no flowers on his desk next to the small, red flag that hopped from the impact.

Wolfgang swore.

"He confided nothing to you?" he yelled, his face twisted with rage. "Do you not understand that there is no time, no time left!"

Gretchen rose slowly from her chair, and, standing straight with unnerving dignity and confidence said:

"Don't be a fool, Wolfy. It took me two weeks to get *you* in bed."

The blood drained from Wolfgang's face.

"If I ask, in two days he will give up his mother to me," added Gretchen.

She turned and walked away from Pfingste's desk.

As she walked away, Pfingste watched the roll of her hips with the thrill and disgust, the excitement and repulsion, the rutting hunger for sex even in men like him who loved their wives. And as the door closed behind Greta or Gretchen or whatever her name was today, Wolfgang knew one thing with absolute certainty.

He smiled weakly and said out loud to himself, "Max Riegelmann is as good as dead. He is a dead man," and he believed it.

Wolfgang plopped into his chair and, with his elbows on the worn fabric of his knees and his face buried in the palms of his hands, he thought of the brutal Russians and the relentless Americans gathering, gathering, gathering, and he added:

"We are *all* dead men."

September 1952, Bowery, New York City

It was cold and the twilight sky was overcast and starless as Leo Rosenbaum finished his shift at his newspaper and walked out of the front door of *Tog Morgen Zhurnal* at 77-79 Bowery. He was dressed in his big coat but without his furry hat and gloves. He had forgotten both that morning and he knew that his old lady would chide him about that when he got home tonight. Leo was a bit absent-minded about commonplace matters.

It was anything but his first walk down the oldest thoroughfare in Gotham; Leo had been born there and had spent his entire life in the wilderness of neon and painted signage, rusting fire escapes, flophouses, cheap bars and restaurants, and retail and wholesale lighting and restaurant fixtures businesses that had become the debauched heart and soul of the Bowery.

He loved and hated what it had become—Gotham's skid row—and, as a reporter, he knew every brick, nook, and cranny, most of the business owners, and almost all of the bums on the street. Leo also knew what his home had once been; he was the resident Bowery historian at the *Zhurnal*. So it almost went without saying that he knew where to find The Admiral. *McGurk's Suicide Hall.*

The reporter thought of Bowery history as he walked on the sidewalk where the poet Walt Whitman once strolled, where minstrelsy, and Jim Crow, and Yiddish Hendricks, and vaudeville and burlesque had been born. In their day, it had been the stomping grounds of the b-hoys and the first gangs in the Big Apple, where the political cancer of Tammany Hall had grown out of its bars, flophouses, cat houses and dives. Now it was a slum; Hell for the destitute, the criminal, and those either forgotten by the world or running from it into alcoholism and drugs. But it was his slum.

In his mind, he pictured the first horse drawn streetcar in America, where Aaron Burr had lived at 129 Bowery in 1833 with his illegitimate son, where P. T. Barnum got his start in 1835 displaying a 161 years old black woman at Chatham Square (she was 80 years old), and of *McGurk's* full of worn out prostitutes who killed themselves there in much less than quiet desperation, giving *McGurk's* its nickname, *Suicide Hall.*

Leo was ruminating over *The London Theater,* long gone and mostly forgotten, where the vaudevillian and movie star W. C. Fields debuted as a juggler, when he saw James Bridges leaning against a wall outside of *McGurk's.*

The reporter waved his arms broadly and shouted: "James! Admiral!" as he approached the black man. "It's me, Lou. Lou Rosenbaum!"

Bridges pushed himself away from the wall, but did not respond. He took a long draw from the cigarette in his mouth, and blew its smoke out.

"How are you doing, 'preacher'?" added Lou and stuck out his hand in greeting.

"It's your old friend, Lou."

"An 'old friend' would know I'm blind and can't see his face," said Bridges. "Just who the Hell are you, really."

"When I was little a kid, I used to be in your congregation back when you were a holy roller. Leo? The little Jewish kid who was a Christian? I've seen you around the Bowery, sometimes. At *Al's, Sammy's,* the bars."

"Leo, Leo, Leo," said Bridges, trying to shake Rosenbaum's memory back into his head. "You don't mean the one whose writing for that Jewish rag? Those stories about the madwoman?"

"Yeah, yeah. That's me, and that's why I'm here, Mr. Bridges. A little bird just told me that you know something about Snake."

Bridges took the cigarette out of his mouth. "I know that they're slimy and bite people. Especially Adam and Eve, metaphorically speaking. Well, well, well, little Leo Rosenbaum. I can't say I'm surprised that you're here. I'm only surprised that it took an Ace Reporter this long."

"Uh, what? Took so long for what?"

It was then that Leo felt the small, hard cylinder press against his spine.

"Don't turn around, newsboy," said a disembodied voice like a racketing, full throated growl behind him. "And keep your hands where I can see them."

"That's Hank," said The Admiral. "He's a friend of mine. If I were you I'd do what he says. Now, why would a smart newshound like you want answers to questions out in the open like this? I think we should step into the alley."

"Sounds right to me, Admiral," said Hank, and poked Leo in the back.

Neither Hank nor The Admiral could see the blood drain from Leo's face.

"Look, guys, you don't want to do this," the reporter said trying to keep his voice from trembling. "If you shoot me here, someone is bound to see and they'll get you both sure as Hell."

"And who's to see, bud?" asked Hank. "If you haven't noticed, there's no one on the sidewalk, Leo. If someone in a passing car should look, they'd see a drunk in front of a Bowery bar slump into my arms. That drunk will be a dead you."

"If you take me into the alley and beat me to a pulp, Hank, that won't stop me. I'm pretty tenacious. If you shoot me, you'll have every reporter in the city breathing down your necks."

"Shut up," said Hank, "and move."

"Alright, alright. Just be careful with that damn thing."

Feeling his way by tapping his cane on the sidewalk, The Admiral, with Leo and Hank following, walked into the mouth of the alley flanking *McGurk's* and stopped. Parked half way down it, a taxi idled, back-lighting and throwing into silhouette three men and one woman standing in front of its headlights. As he neared them, details began to emerge out of the silhouettes.

When Leo hesitated, Hank poked him in the back with the gun. "Get going."

As he stumbled forward, the four silhouettes came into complete focus and the reporter recognized Jack Flash from *Sammy's Bowery Follies*, Ham, the massive bouncer from the same bar, and a third, very tall and skinny man he had never seen before that night dressed like a cheap burlesque magician in a tattered suit with tails and a top hat. He would later learn that his name was Alfonso Longfellow.

Jack was grinning like the madman he was, his paddle cradled in his arms like a rifle, Ham was smacking an iron pipe into his opened right palm, and the third thug was cracking his knuckles. The fourth, Typhoid Mary, was counting the links in a heavy chain with her left hand as if she were counting the beads in a rosary.

"So, you're not going to kill me," said Leo.

"We oughtta, ya know," said Typhoid. "He's a lousy tipper."

"Oh, ye of little faith," said The Admiral. "Show him, Hank."

Hank stepped around and in front of the reporter. He raised his right hand that mocked the shape of a gun up to his lips and blew imaginary smoke from his forefinger.

Jack Flash slapped the blade of his paddle on the concrete and said, "Bang!" and then did it a second time, and said, "Bang! Bang! You're dead!"

"You see, Leo, it's this way," said The Admiral. "We're all snitches for the 'madwoman' you call Snake because, well, she can't be everywhere at once and she needs to know certain things, considering the business she's in. We're her eyes and ears.

"I'm guessing you've figured out by now that we knew you were coming tonight? Remember, eyes and ears everywhere?

"You know Jack. You don't need to know the tall one right now. The big guy with the lead pipe. That's Ham. I think you've met him. He's taken to calling us operatives the 'Nest of Vipers'. These guys are here to protect Hank and me. We watch each others' backs all the time."

"Oh my G-god," Leo stammered, fighting, but failing, to control his fear. "There's only one reason you'd be telling me all of this.

"You *are* going to kill me."

"Ya think?" said Bridges.

"Get going."

Chapter Five

Berlin, November, 1944

Greta gently touched the outer edge of the ornate, iron, Art Deco picture frame as she looked wistfully at a photograph of herself and her sister when they were twelve years old—all pony tails, ribbons, and smiles. Fresh and refreshed from a shower, she stood in front of her chest-of-drawers in her apartment in comfortable, Chinese, silk pajamas with a coiled cobra painted over her left breast. She wore them because they felt wonderful on her cool, clean, pink skin, and she liked to feel good. Her wet, brown hair cascaded in strands.

On the wall behind the chest-of-drawers was mounted a grouping of four Kabuki masks made of porcelain; a laughing blue mask, a yellow mask of fear, a blue one of sorrow, and a white mask of indifference.

Her tortoise-shell cat, Dolly, lay half-asleep, curled on her couch.

Germany's greatest spy touched the pads of two fingers to her lips and then touched her sister's image with them leaving a thin, small and temporary fog. Then she straightened, padded across her carpeted floor on bare feet to a small, decorative table where her phonograph player rested, and opened its dark, cherry-wood lid. A long-playing vinyl disc of recordings of several of Beethoven's works lay on the turntable. Greta turned the record player on and placed its phonographic needle on the disc. The melancholy chords of her favorite song, *Für Elise*. swelled up and filled the room.

She stood in front of the phonograph player for several moments with her eyes closed and her lips barely parted. Then she raised her slender arms, her hands loose, and she performed a plie with all of the grace and beauty of a ballerina performing to an adoring, invisible audience. She repeated her plie, then spun around like a falling leaf caught in a breeze. She took a deep breath, shook relaxation into the muscles of her body, and slowly began to dance.

The scope and speed of her dancing increased as Greta lost herself in Beethoven's rich, moody orchestration and the Plie, Arabesque, and Tendu of ballet came easily, without conscious effort, the product of years of study as a child. Then the formal, graceful movements of ballet morphed into ballroom dancing as she held and was held, held and released, held and was held by an imaginary Fred Astaire as her partner. Her furniture became choreographed props as she and Astaire spun like a whirlwind around her couch, leapt with the grace of a gazelle over an ottoman, and overturned and danced over a chair as they moved faster, faster, and effortlessly through the East Coast Swag, the Linde Hop, an Impressionistic Waltz, Foxtrot, and finally the wild, breathless abandon of Free Style.

Finally exhausted, Greta fell back into her overstuffed chair as the final chords of *Für Elise* fell silent. Breathing deeply, full of joy and satiated, she almost laughed. Then as her breathing regulated and her heart slowed, her smile faded and her eyes fixed on something beyond her apartment, beyond Berlin and Germany, beyond space and time.

And Greta buried her face in the palms of her hands and wept like a baby.

Their Sunday afternoon drive to a forest on the outskirts of Berlin in Max's black roadster was a rare luxury; one had to either be a Nazi elite or a valued Nazi commodity to get rationed gasoline now. Even though it was only one o'clock and the sky was clear and the weather unseasonably warm, they had passed few other vehicles as the trees flickered outside the roadster's windows like the pages of a flip book. The hrmmmm of the tires on the concrete was almost mesmerizing and only added to a somber feeling of melancholy and an unspoken anticipation by the surgeon that Max Riegelmann and Gretchen Lagle were on the cusp of a national catastrophe.

Max wore a light, leather jacket over his best Sunday suit and a Bowler hat, and Gretchen sat next to him on the bench seat in a blue jacket over a flowery dress, simple leather shoes, and white gloves. A wicker picnic basket sat on the seat between Gretchen and the passenger's door.

"You aren't like the other women I've known before," said Max as he glanced at the flickering trees through the window on the driver's side of the roadster. "You're so easy to talk to, so easy to be around, Gretchen."

"You're just being silly, Maxey," Gretchen cooed and placed her soft, cool, right hand on his forearm. "I'm just like any other girl. I want the same things any girl wants. I have the same hopes and dreams. Marriage someday, and a family."

"No. No, that's not true. I'm an...ugly man, Gretchen, and a little man, but you treat me like I'm normal."

"Don't start that again, sweetheart. Everyone has little things about them that they don't like. Me included. Some mornings, I can't even bare to look at myself in the mirror. Not enough of what I should have in one place; too much in another. You have to learn to count your blessings."

"I do count my blessings. I have one, and that's you."

"Oh, Max. That's so sweet. When you say things like that, it makes me feel like a million dollars. But please don't put me up on a pedestal. I'll fall off for sure.

"I made bratwurst on Kaiser rolls for our picnic today, with pickles and mustard. And I brought a couple of nice bottles of beer. All the things you like, sweetheart. Is it much further?"

Even as she spoke, Max began to slow the speed of the roadster and pull over to the shoulder of the road next to the forest, its brittle, denuded fingers like a tangled mass of other, spider-webbed fingers reaching to the sky.

"This is it, Fraulein. This is where I come to walk and think about things. Sometimes, I bring a book to read. I'm sorry it's not exactly beautiful right now. Just a short walk in is a clearing where I like to sit and read."

"It must be lovely in the spring," said Gretchen as the car rolled to a stop. "I can just imagine the leaves of so many different colors and the flowers. Can we some back in the spring, darling?"

Max did not answer. The doors to the roadster opened. The surgeon stepped out, stretched his arms and arched his back as Gretchen lifted the basket out of the car and closed her door. In a heartbeat, Gretchen, almost gay, and Max, even smiling a bit, were walking hand-in-hand into the brittle, winter forest.

"How did you find this place? Have you brought another girl here?" Gretchen asked as they strolled, sharing the inane and light conversation of lovers lost in one another. "Have you come here for a long time, Maxey?"

"There have been no other girls, Gretchen. Remember?"

The almost forgotten picnic basket hanging in the crook of her right arm bumped against her thigh to the rhythm and sway of her hips. A light breeze made her long red hair dance around her neck.

"Actually, my mom and dad used to bring us here when they were alive."

"I certainly hope so. A picnic would have been a real hardship *after* they died."

There was a pause as Gretchen hid her whimsical smile with several fingers and the light of understanding dawned on Max. He began to chuckle.

"You know, sweetheart, I think that's the first time I've heard you laugh!"

"Now that we're together, it won't be the last," grinned Max as they suddenly stepped out of the forest and onto the edge of the promised clearing—a space of no more than twenty feet in diameter that the season had cleared of weeds. A fallen and slowly rotting tree trunk lay on the ground at the side opposite from the couple.

"We're here!" Max exclaimed, and pulled his girl eagerly forward.

"It's just lovely. Are you hungry?" asked Gretchen as they approached the trunk.

"Famished," Max said, his eyes only on his beloved.

In a second heartbeat, he stopped, turned suddenly to Gretchen, and kissed her. She put her free arm around his neck, and returned his kiss passionately. Just as quickly, he released her and she released him, and he lowered his face and blushed.

"I'm s-sorry. I...just...couldn't help myself," he stammered.

"I liked it!" bubbled Gretchen, and pulling him by the hand, added, "Come on, sweetheart. Let's have some fun!"

Four steps brought the couple to the fallen log. Max's eyes never left Gretchen as he turned his back on the trunk and began to sit.

"Max!" yelled Gretchen. "Maxey!"

The surgeon straightened, bewildered.

"What...?"

"Look," said Gretchen, and pointed with her free hand. "On the trunk!"

Max followed the direction of her arm to see a small snake, curled into a tight ball, sunning itself on the trunk where he would have sat.

He yelped involuntarily as he stumbled back. The snake awoke and reared its head. The blood drained from Max's face. His eyes welled with tears, and his entire body began to shake. Gretchen dropped the picnic basket and grabbed his bicep with both of her hands.

"Max?" she said. "Max, honey. What's wrong? I didn't mean to frighten you. It's only a harmless little snake."

He tried to pull away from her as, flicking its tongue; the snake slithered down the trunk and disappeared beneath it.

"I-I can't, I can't, I can't," he whispered, his eyes fixed on something beyond the here and now, into the reality of a past childhood horror.

Gretchen followed but restrained him from leaving the clearing at the edge of the forest opposite the tree trunk.

"It's alright now, honey. It's alright," she began to console him as a calculating smile that he did not see began to curl her lips. She laid the soft, cool palm of her right hand against his left cheek. His cheek was damp.

"It can't reach us here. We're safe here. Look. Look, it's gone. Now, just take a few, slow breaths, and calm down, sweetheart. It was only a garden snake."

Max followed her instruction and slowed his breathing until his face began to drain of blood again. He focused on Gretchen.

"You don't understand," he said, almost in a whisper, full of the shame that only a man can understand. "I know it's unreasonable, but I've had an illogical fear of snakes, all snakes, any snake, ever since I was a little boy."

"I understand, Maxey. We're all afraid of something. I'm afraid of spiders. Why don't you just take a moment and tell me about it, sweetheart."

"My brother, Franz, and I used to play in the garden just behind our house when we were seven years old, I think," began Max.

"Franz? You have a brother named Franz?" asked Gretchen. "You've never said a word about him until now. Does he live in Germany? Maybe even Berlin? I'd like to meet him someday."

"Yes. Yes. We are actually fraternal twins, although Franz is almost the exact opposite of me physically. Anyway, I was seven, I think, as was he. I remember it was a bright warm day in the spring, and we used to play soldiers and spacemen and Vikings in our garden when mama would let us."

"What a wonderful picture that has put in my mind. I wish I had known you then, Maxey. You must have been a darling little boy."

"No, Gretchen, Not really, So, uh, one day, we were playing at something, I can't remember what, and I bent down to pick up what I thought was a stick on the ground to use as a sword."

"It was a s-s-snake."

Gretchen saw his face blanch again, and she squeezed his bicep for assurance.

"It was a long time ago," she cooed. "And you were so young, darling."

"It was a little one, and it must have been as frightened of me as I was of it, but I, uh, didn't know that, and it bit me on the pad of the index finger of my right hand. It hurt like Hell, and I'm ashamed to say that I panicked and tried to shake it off while I was screaming bloody murder."

"It was my twin brother, Franz, who finally pulled the s-snake off."

"I've never forgotten that day, and even though, as an adult, I know it wasn't really all that big a deal, I have never been able to get over the memory. I have been terrified of s-s-snakes ever since."

"My favorite author is the American, Mark Twain, sweetheart. I remember that he wrote something like 'courage is resistance to fear, the mastery of fear — not absence of fear'. Being afraid of a snake when you were a little boy doesn't make you a coward."

But being afraid when you're a man certainly makes you a sniveling little coward now, she thought in her mind.

"I am so ashamed. I must look like a coward and a fool to you,"

Gretchen took Max's face between both of her cool hands, and looked him squarely in his eyes.

"You look nothing of the kind, darling, What you are is an intelligent man who sees more than just my body when he looks at me, who talks to me like an equal, who treats me with kindness, and gentleness, and...love."

Then Gretchen brought his face to hers and, melting her body against him, kissed him passionately on the lips.

It seemed an eternity of bliss before she drew back and said, "Now, put this out of your mind, darling. As far as I'm concerned, it never happened. I'll go get our basket, and we'll just sit in the car and have our picnic. Is that okay?"

"Yes. Yes, that would be alright."

Max threw his arms around her and embraced her. Gretchen returned his embrace with all of the passion and submission of a woman in love.

"Gretchen, Gretchen, Gretchen, I brought you here to tell you something that no one else must hear," Max said, and buried his face in the cascading waves of her silken hair at her neck.

"Why don't you walk back to the car while I get the picnic basket, and you can tell me while we eat, sweetheart. We have all the time in the world."

"Yes, while we eat," Max said, still shaken, and, releasing her, he turned and walked into the forest.

He was sitting on the passenger's side of the car with both of its door open when Gretchen came out of the forest carrying her basket. She waved at him and smiled as she approached. He returned her wave and scooted across the bench seat to sit behind the steering wheel.

"There's my favorite guy in the whole world," she said, now framed in the open door of the roadster. She sat the picnic basket on the seat next to Max and sat down next to it. "Are you feeling any better?"

"Better," he mumbled.

"You still look awfully anxious, honey. Do you need a few more minutes before we eat? Do you feel up to talking some more about it? I'm real good at listening."

"It's not that, Gretchen," he answered, unable to mask the anxious tone of his voice. Max leaned across the picnic basket as she turned to face him and took both of her shoulders in his clammy hands.

"I can't live without you," he whispered, holding her gently by her shoulders. "And I'm afraid for you...and for myself. I brought you here today for more than a picnic. I brought you hear to talk to you in complete privacy."

"What do you mean, darling? Is something wrong? Did I mess up something back at the office? If I did..."

"No Gretchen," Max interrupted. "Nothing is wrong at the office. No one can hear us now, so I can speak freely. I know that you must see what I see as well, that the Allied forces are winning and Germany is on the verge of collapse..."

"Max!" interrupted Gretchen, shocked at his words. "Surely you don't really mean that? Germany is destined to rule the world!"

"There's no need to pretend anymore. No need to pretend with me. I've seen it coming for some time and I've made...arrangements. We've got to get out of Germany."

He stopped her next words with the index and middle fingers of his right hand pressed carefully over her lips.

"There's no need to say anymore right now, but I just want you to know that...that I love you and need you and will not let Hitler and the Nazis destroy what I have waited for all of my life...you. Please. Say you'll come with me if and when the time comes."

Gretchen returned his look of love and passion with one of her own.

"I'm not sure I understand, but I will go wherever you go, Max.

"I...I love you too."

"Oh, Gretchen, Gretchen! I'm the happiest man alive!"

"And I'm the happiest woman. Now, we need to slow down and compose ourselves. Why don't you just take a long, quiet breath and talk about something else. Why don't you tell me all about your brother, Franz."

It was at that tender, vulnerable moment that the hunchbacked surgeon who had lived most of his lonely life ostracized and on the fringe of society, who had ached for friendship, acceptance, and the touch of a woman, who had numbed his isolation by losing himself in books and medicine, poured out his heart to Gretchen and made the two greatest mistakes of his entire life.

He told Gretchen about Franz.

And he told her about everything.

September 1952, Bowery, New York City

The light was blinding.

Leo jerked his hands up to cup his eyes, only slowly lowering them as vague outlines began to gather into distinct forms between his protective fingers and his eyes became accustomed to the light.

Hank, the hack, stood directly in front of the reporter, grinning around a cigarette. He was holding the blindfold that he had just removed from Rosenbaum's face.

"Well, well, well, bud" said the cabbie, "I told ya you weren't dead."

Leo said nothing as he took a quick survey of the small room where he found himself a prisoner. Because he'd been no more than five minutes or so in the vehicle that had brought him to this undisclosed location, he knew he was still somewhere in or near the Bowery. Because of the shoddy condition of the sparsely furnished room—the wallpaper was fading and tattered, there was dust everywhere, and there was even cardboard taped over the transom over the front door and the windows to blind them—he also surmised that he was either in an abandoned tenement or an unused and neglected office over a business on the thoroughfare. He could hear no city noise although it was still early evening, and from the stagnant air, Max also knew the room was neither heated nor air conditioned. Not that any of that really mattered, since he would soon be dead.

He coughed nervously.

Hank blocked his view somewhat, but the reporter saw The Admiral seated in a metal folding chair to the cabbie's left side, also smoking a ciga-rette. The elderly black man held a large manila envelope in his left hand. So the only question left him was whether the woman in the Kabuki mask with a painted cobra on its left cheek and wearing an outrageous leather costume standing to the right of Hank would be the one who butchered him.

"Where am I?" Leo asked.

"Curiouser and curiouser," cooed an eerie voice like the hissing of a snake behind the Kabuki mask. "I thought reporters were supposed to know everything. For instance, did you know, Mr. Reporter, that the two most important days of your life are the day you are born—and the day you find out why. Well, blow me down!"

"What is that supposed to mean?" Leo asked, and took two steps back from the other, leather-clad she-devil. That was when he noticed the snake-headed quarterstaff in her right hand and the blacksnake whip on her left hip and the gun that Hank was pointing at his chest.

"It means whatever she wants it to mean," said Hank, and waved his gun to his left, inviting Leo to sit in a second, empty folding chair. "She likes to babble on sometimes. Now, show the lady a little respect, and park it."

"Thanks, but I don't feel like sitting. I'm late getting home and my wife is expecting me. I've gotta leave now."

The Kabuki mask hissed: "Nothing of importance ever happens to us after we reach the age of twelve. Sit down, please."

Leo studied the she with a body that makes men ache and knew that the reports in his competitor's newspapers were right—this woman was certifiably as crazy as the Mad Hatter in Wonderland.

She said it again, and her voice was ice. "Sit...down. This is not a game, Mr. Rosenbaum, and neither are you dreaming. You have found what you have long sought, my Nest of Vipers. And, frankly my dear, I don't give a damn."

"He doesn't understand, yet," said The Admiral to the madwoman, "that he's being handed the story of his lifetime on a silver platter, honey. I told you he wasn't the brightest candle in the menorah."

"I'm Leo Rosenbaum," the reporter said as he reluctantly sat. "I'm a reporter for the *Tog Morgen Zhurnal* newspaper in the Bowery."

"I know who you are, but who am I," said the Kabuki mask, as Snake began to pace back and forth in front of the reporter. "The quick green dragon ate the highway with its stained glass teeth. Shazam!" "You'll have to excuse her. She has lucid days and crazy bad days," said The Admiral. "On one of the really bad ones, she babbles in German. Little Leo, it looks like we caught you on one of her crazy ones."

"Who are you?" said Leo, ignoring the blind black man. "You are the one that we are calling Snake because of that quarterstaff you carry; the vigilante who robs from thieves and doesn't give to the poor."

"Who in the world am I?" said Snake, tapping the head of her quarterstaff into the palm of her open left hand. "Ah, that's the great puzzle. I can't explain myself, I'm afraid, sir, because I'm not myself, you see. I yam what I yam and that's all that I yam! But come back tomorrow and you may be me!"

"When she's like this," said The Admiral, "I sorta act as the spokesperson for the Nest, Leo. You are here because she reads the *Zhurnal* among a half a dozen other newspapers, and, for some mysterious reason, likes your style. So she has a proposition for you.

"It isn't a complicated one. You have quick access to information that could benefit us a great deal. So, tonight, you will become one of us, a snitch, little Leo, or... Hank can place a carefully aimed bullet between your eyes."

"What?" asked Leo.

"As a valued member of our little Nest of Vipers, you will forward any information you get about upcoming criminal activity in the Bowery to Snake. We'll show you how. In return and as a start, she will allow you to publish an actual photo of her—I have it right here in this envelope just waiting for a home on the front page of your newspaper—making you an instant very big deal in the world of Gotham newspapers, and in the future she'll give you exclusive information about *all* of her...activities."

"What is the use of a newspaper," said the vigilante—the snake's head of her quarterstaff slapped into her palm—"without pictures or conversations? Hot dog!"

"So, what's it going to be, Leo?" asked The Admiral, and waved the large envelope as proof of the legitimacy of his offer. "Fame or your wife becomes a widow?"

"Twinkle, twinkle, little bat!" said Snake, "how I wonder what you're at? We have met the enemy and he is us."

"This is crazy," said Leo, rising from his chair. "And I won't do it, and you won't kill me because that would bring every reporter and cop in the City down on your...!"

Hank fired his gun *BANG* into the ceiling.

"This is insane," said Leo as he watched the cabbie lower his gun and aim it at his face. "This is nuts! She's stark raving mad! This can't be happening!"

"We're all mad here," said The Admiral. "So...that's a no?"

"Oh, my ears and whiskers, it's getting late" said Snake, and threw back her head and laughed. "Always do right. This will gratify some people and astonish the rest."

Wide-eyed and trembling, Leo looked at Hank and the hack's gun pointed at his head, and then at The Admiral, offering him the envelope, and then at the mad woman in the outrageous leather costume who was laughing and clutching her stomach with her free hand.

He took the envelope.

Snake stopped laughing and sang, "Happy trails to you until we meet again."

Leo Rosenbaum, the self-anointed ace reporter for the *Zhurnal*, the husband of one wife and father of no children, fell heavily into his easy chair in his modest apartment. He heard his wife, Annabel, who was long familiar and resigned to his odd hours as a reporter, rummaging in the kitchen.

"I'm home!" he said, and looked intently for several moments at the manila envelope in his hand.

"Be right there, honey," answered his wife.

Hank and The Admiral had dropped him off at the mouth of the same alley where they had kidnapped him. The long walk home had given the reporter plenty of time to ponder his options. He could join the self-pro-claimed Nest of Vipers, scoop every other reporter in The Big Apple with story after story about the mysterious leather-clad she-devil who stole from thieves, and eventually earn himself a position at the prestigious New York Times—that and winning the Pulitzer were the ultimate goals of his life—and, by becoming Snake's snitch, he would also become what he hated most, one of the thugs and slime who made life in the City a mis-ery for many and meant death for a few.

Annabel appeared in the doorway to the kitchen dressed in a simple, striped dress with her short, brown hair in a ponytail and slightly in dis-array.

She asked: "How was your day, honey?"

Or, Leo continued to ruminate, he could just publish the photograph of the leather-clad madwoman, do his job, and let the cards fall where they may, so to speak. He reasoned that if he'd seen the entire Nest, they weren't exactly legion in number, and he could probably survive with his skin still attached by just doing his job. But, then, if he didn't turn Snake and her Nest of Vipers into the police, he became a de facto criminal himself. Or he could do the right thing and call his long-time buddy, Lieutenant Sam Manning at the 9th precinct, probably forfeiting that job at the Times.

Annabel repeated, "How was your day, honey? Is something wrong?"

"What? Oh? Sorry sugar cookie," Leo responded and quickly moved the envelope in his hand behind his back. "Just a lot on my mind, I guess. How was your day?"

"Just find, Leo." Annabel was fully in the living room now and fully engaged in the moment. "What's that you're holding behind your back?"

"What," Leo blushed, and brought forth the envelope. "This? Just more homework for a story I'm working on for the paper."

He tossed the envelope on the top of a small table next to his recliner.

Annabel was neither beautiful nor homely, with a narrow face, high cheekbones that were always slightly roughed, and modest lips—most people would not have noticed her in a crowd— but she swept up to Leo with an unconscious grace, charm, and vulnerability born from a long heritage of women who had selflessly given their lives to the men they loved, and threw her arms around his neck and kissed him.

"We got a letter from Aunt Helen today. Little Will is feeling much bet-ter."

"Good," Leo answered as Annabel released him and stepped several feet back from her husband. "That's good. Anything else happen today?"

"You're only half paying attention to me. You're all stressed out again, aren't you, Leo? Don't lie to me, honey. You were never a good liar."

"No, no, no. Out of the unusual, nothing."

"You know you can leave that paper any time you want. Uncle Levi said he has a job open for you anytime you want it. All you have to do is ask."

Annabel had his attention, now. She smiled.

"On that again, let's not start eh? I'm tired and hungry."

"Good. We're having a nice piece of halibut I got fresh from the butcher today, sweetheart, and I made mashed potatoes and green beans for supper. Nothing much else. You do look tired, honey. Go ahead. Sit down."

The reporter snuggled back in his favorite chair, huffed, and looked up at his wife. He had decided on his somber walk home that he'd go to the police in the morning before checking in at work. So, emotionally and physically exhausted, he picked up the envelope from the desk and opened it as Annabel turned to leave the room.

Rosenblum shook out its contents into his right hand. There was a posed picture of Snake in full leather regalia and mask and three, crisp, one hundred dollar bills—more than his salary for a month.

"Supper will be on in a jiff," Annabel said, her spirits lifted again as she neared the kitchen doorway. With her back to her husband, and half-way through that doorway, Annabel added: "Honey, I almost forgot. Someone stopped by earlier to see you. I didn't get his name but his business card is on the table next to you."

Leo looked at the little end-table next to his chair and saw and picked up the card that was lying face down next to the small lamp there. His face drained of blood. He looked up from the card at his wife now standing in the kitchen doorway, obviously genuinely glad that he was home.

"Funny thing," she said, smiling. "There was no name on the card. Just a...."

Leo let the card drop from his hand.

On the card was the image of a striking Cobra.

Chapter Six

Berlin, November, 1944

T he door to Max's apartment splintered under the jackboot and slammed back against the interior wall of his living room. Sitting in his favorite chair, Max looked up from the book he was reading. Like a clot of blood, the Nazi SS bled through the breached doorway with weapons drawn.

On the first day of endless pain and torture, several of Max Rosenbaum's teeth had squirted from his split lips and scattered like tossed pebbles across the floor. The hump on his naked back had been flayed into an uneven grid of bloody welts left by the bite of a leather bullwhip that had carried away bits of his lacerated flesh.

Max had been stripped to the waist, and his wrists had been rubbed raw and bloody from the twisted hemp rope that bound them behind the back of a slatted, wooden chair, the only furnishing in a tiny, windowless and unvented room that had been made more claustrophobic by the presence of five Nazi SS thugs. As Max had slumped in the chair, his head had lolled to his left shoulder as if his neck had been broken; it had not been broken. The surgeon's face had been cut, bruised, burned, and become tumescent; his left eye had swollen shut.

"You will talk," said Karl Von Aspe of the Schutzstaffell who, also stripped to his waist, had stood in front of Max with his gloved, balled fists on his hips. Both he, Max, and the other four Nazi had swum in sweat from the oppressive heat in the tiny interrogation room.

"Despite your denials," his tormentor had said, "we know you're a member of the *Sieg*, a traitor to your *Führer*, the Fatherland, and our people. We know about your brother, Franz, and the plot to assassinate Adolph. We are torturing your beloved brother right now in this very building. But what maybe you don't understand yet, yes? Is that you will not leave this room...alive...unless and until you tell me the names of the other *Sieg* traitors and where they are hiding. Do you understand me, doctor?"

Max had said nothing.

"I must admit, your tenacity has surprised me somewhat," Von Aspe had said and he had snapped his fingers. The Nazi thug closest to the entrance to the room had nodded, opened the door, and left, slamming the door behind him. "But we have more than tenacity. We have Right on our side, and you will talk!"

Max had sputtered, "Go...to...Hell."

"I thought you Jews didn't believe in Hell," his tormentor had said and smiled. "Oh, well, it doesn't really matter."

The door to the room had opened again, closed again, and the same Nazi who had left a moment before was now carrying a long, lidded, wooden box punctured with holes under his left arm. He had moved quickly to his leader and handed him the container.

"Clean him up," Von Aspe had commanded.

One of his fellow SS men then swung a small bucket full of water that splashed in Max's face. Sputtering and gasping for breath, Max had lowered his head to just inches above his chest and opened his one good eye.

"Now is the time for you to pray to your God," Von Aspe had barked as he opened the lid to the box. "Now is the time for you to beg for forgiveness, to confess your sins, Max Rieglemann. Now is the time for you to confront your worst horror!"

So saying and clutching it just behind its green, wedge-shaped head, Karl had pulled a snake from the box and dangled its seven foot long writhing body in front of what little was left physically and emotionally of the famous surgeon to the Nazis.

Max had screamed and struggled frantically against his ropes.

Lashing madly in response to his screams, the snake then wrapped itself around Karl's forearm as the Nazi had leaned close to Max's face and pinched the flesh just behind the viper's jaws.

"I'd like you to meet our little pet." The snake had bared its white fangs. "We call him Satan."

Max had screamed and screamed in almost insane horror as his tormentor now held the snake's head only inches from the surgeon's face.

Then Max had spat in Von Aspe's face.

The brutal, relentless, monstrous beating that had followed left Von Aspe red-faced and gasping for breath and reduced Max to a bloody inhuman mass of delirious pain that no man could long endure and live.

The door to Franz Rieglmann's room inside an abandoned warehouse splintered under Konrad Schlossbein's polished, black jackboot. Sitting on a cot against the wall furthest from the door and writing in a notebook propped on his thigh, Franz looked up. Like a clot of blood, the Nazi Schutzstaffell and his fellow SS Men, bled through the ruptured doorway with their weapons drawn and aimed at his torso.

"Go…to…Hell."

As Max suffered the horrifying consequences of spitting in the face of his Nazi torturer, Franz Rieglmann slumped, bound to a chair and stripped naked to the waist, in a tiny room three floors beneath his brother. Battered and almost comatose, he fell in and out of consciousness. His once hard, muscular, powerful torso honed in the military ranks of the Nazis was peppered with angry, red craters burned into his flesh by a lit cigar, and had been further torn to ribbons in an uneven grid of bloody swastikas left from the sting of a red-hot iron rod that had carried away bits of his lacerated flesh with each branding. Pig's fat was smeared over his glistening, naked flesh in the mistaken belief that Franz was an orthodox Jew and would be humiliated and outraged by such sacrilege.

Konrad Schlossbein was not without a sadistic sense of humor.

As Franz twisted weakly against his bonds on his small, metal, folding chair, his chin turned to his left shoulder in an irrational gesture of defiance, his face cut, bruised, burned, and tumescent, no tears welled in his eyes or fell down his torn cheeks.

Konrad stood with his back to three of his Nazi cohorts and facing Franz, shifting his weight impatiently from his left to his right foot, and then back again, slapped the flat edge of the blade of a large sword into the palm of his right, gloved hand. Great half-moons of sweat stained his uniform beneath both of his armpits. The glove was wet with Franz's blood.

"You stinking Jewish pig," Konrad spat. "You will give up the names of your other *Sieg* co-conspirators just as your yellow brother gave you up, or you will die today!

Barely above a whisper, Franz said, "You lie."

One of Konrad's thugs took a threatening step forward, his hand on a gun at his hip, but Konrad stopped him with a raised hand.

"Only when necessary to forward the cause of our *Führer*," he said, and leaned close to Franz's brutalized face. His own face was red from exertion, wet with sweat, unshaven, and burned from the sun. "It doesn't have to be this way. The beating, I mean. The burning. All of this. I could free you and spare the life of your brother as well with one spoken word. You may rest assured; I have that kind of authority, Franz. Wouldn't it be better for you and your brother to live out your lives in jail than to die today? Just tell me their names and where they are hiding."

"I...would rather...die," Franz gasped, then choked on his own blood for a moment. "...than live with the Nazi heel on my throat."

Konrad straightened. He brandished his sword at an invisible opponent only inches from the left side of Franz's face. "Very well," he said, casually. "As you wish," Konrad added and swung the sword and his body as far to his left as was possible and still maintain his balance.

"Gentlemen," he said, addressing the three other SS thugs in the room, "maybe we can loosen Max's tongue by loosening his."

Konrad swung the blade with all of his strength and weight. There was the sucking sound of a butcher's knife cutting meat.

Franz's head rolled kathunk kathunk kathunk unevenly across the floor leaving a smear of blood to rest against a black, spit-polished Nazi jackboot.

On the second day, Max hung from the same chair as if crucified in the same sweltering room and bound by the same ropes filthy with his Jewish blood, more dead than alive, babbling under his breath about a well full of writhing snakes.

The door to the room opened, and Karl Von Aspe entered in full Nazi regalia with one of his flunkies carrying a bucket. He was meticulously groomed and carried what looked like a hat box for a man.

"Gooood morning, Max Rosenblum!" he said. "I hope you slept well last night because I have wonderful news for you today that will forever change your life."

Von Aspe waved a hand at his cohort who promptly swung his bucket backwards and then forwards, drenching Max with cold water.

Max weakly shook his head like a dog to clear the vision of his one un-swollen eye, and looked up. There were three Von Aspe's standing in front of him.

"The *Führer* himself has sent you a gift," continued Von Aspe as his co-hort took several steps back from him and then laid the bucket on the floor.

Max said nothing as the three Von Aspes became one.

"Adolph has gifted you with one more chance to reveal the names of your fellow *Sieg* traitors and even sent something…special…to help loosen your tongue."

The Nazi thug behind him stifled a snigger with his left hand.

Karl Von Aspe sat the hat box on Max's lap and opened the lid.

He said, "Surprise!"

Max looked down.

Franz looked up as Max looked down.

As Max screamed, Gretchen lay in a luxurious, soapy, claw-footed, por-celain tub in the bathroom of her apartment several miles away. Her red wig rested on the sink. The lights were low, a fluffy, white robe was draped like a snow drop over the closed lid of the toilet, her cat lay curled on the robe, the tub was full of warm, scented water and wreathed with lit, scented candles liberated from the French and gifted by a grateful Colonel to Gretchen. A glass of chilled French Champagne sat near her right hand on the edge of the tub.

It had been a good day. A very good day. She had been richly rewarded. Gretchen's eyes were closed.

She was smiling as she listened to Beethoven's *Funeral March #1.*

Chapter Seven

The belief that there is no absolute truth is a statement of absolute truth and is therefore self-defeating. Only an idiot could believe such a thing. Hitler believed it. Adolph only believed in expediency.
I believed in Hitler. Therefore, I was his idiot.

September 1952, Bowery, New York City

The blindfold fell in his lap.

Dr. Joesph Eacobacci's lumberjack body seemed incongruous in the leather, tufted chair where he sat in a small, windowless room replete with middle class furnishings. He unconsciously stroked his Fu Manchu mustache with his left hand as he took inventory of this, the latest of a half-dozen undisclosed locations that had been chosen for his clandestine meetings with the notorious woman without a name. From a 1930s Zenith console radio standing near his chair, Les Paul's lightning fast fingers were playing "Meet Mr. Callaghan" low and beautifully on his newfangled electric guitar.

Eacobacci wore a simple, black suit bought off of a rack and a grey shirt without a tie. His trademark sunglasses were perched well back on top of his head, and under the left side of his coat, his pearl handled revolver was tucked into the waist of his slacks. He held a small, spiral bound notebook in his right hand with an ink pen clipped to its cover.

"Good morning," the psychologist said, removing the pen from the cover of the notebook. "I hope I find you well today. I notice none of your... associates...has stayed for our session. Does that mean you're beginning to trust me somewhat?"

"Here's lookin' at you, kid," answered the woman behind the Kabuki mask, "'cause you sure ain't lookin' at the real me. Did you eat the Breakfast of Champions today, doctor? Did you eat your Wheaties?"

Eacobacci thought: *she's Humphrey Bogart now?*

She lay with her arm draped over one of the arms of a couch with her left leg extended down its length and her right leg raised at the crook of her knee. Open next to her arm was a copy of a pulp magazine, *Planet Stories,* featuring a blonde bimbo in a low-cut, blue dress and a glass bubble helmet with her ray gun raised and ready to fire. The sexy blonde fronted an alien creature that looked like a cross between a bulldog and a fish with serrated teeth. Except for the Kabuki mask, Snake looked like a normal, healthy woman relaxing after vigorous exercise.

"What's that you're reading?"

"Classic," she said. "Runs the gamut of emotions from A to B, doctor. Twenty years from now you will be more disappointed by the things that you didn't do than by the ones you did do."

Eacobacci tried again. "Aren't you dressed in what I believe is called a sweatsuit today? That certainly shows some progress. I mean, you can't wear leather all of the time!" He opened his notebook and wrote.

He took a second quick inventory of her immediate vicinity before adding, "And no weapons today! Now, isn't that more comfortable than that leather clown's suit you parade around in as 'Snake'?"

"I was born when you kissed me," said Snake. "I died when you left me. I lived a few weeks when you loved me. It's Howdy Doody time!"

Struggling to hide his irritation, the psychologist nevertheless huffed. Eacobacci prided himself in possessing the patience of Job, but he reasoned that her affectation of responding to any question with a non-sequitur, and those as quotes from someone famous or infamous, would have driven even Freud to tear his hair out by the roots.

"I recently read in the *Zhurnal* that you nearly beat a gangster to death in a bar. Carlos Valentine of the DeSalvio family? They'll try to kill you now, you know."

She answered, "The only reason to have money is to tell any SOB to go to Hell. Don't you agree, Doctor Freud? There has been much tragedy in my life; at least half of it actually happened."

The psychologist shook his head in disappointment.

"We have met no few times now, and it seems that I have done nothing to convince you that unless I can talk to the real you without the quotes, I will be unable to help you."

"Things are never so bad," she quoted Bogart, "that they can't be made worse. The past may not repeat itself, but it sure does rhyme. Would you like a nice cup of molasses, doctor? It's good for what ails ya."

Peeved, the psychologist stood up abruptly and, knitting his hands behind his back, began to pace a short path back and forth in front of the reclining woman. After some moments, he stopped just as abruptly in front of the couch.

"I have patiently tried to help you as a way to show my gratitude for saving my daughter. But it is time that I speak bluntly. All else has failed.

"My initial diagnosis of your multiple psychoses—among them your persistent and aberrant use of quotes from others to hide or suppress or even replace your own personality, your robbing your fellow thieves, your propensity for violence, your outlandish clothing—my initial diagnosis, as I was saying, was that these outward acts stem from an inward self-hatred and loathing so intense, so deep rooted, that you wanted to suppress or even replace your true nature to escape yourself by becoming someone else entirely. I surmised that that deep a level of self-loathing must come from an intense feeling of guilt, or shame, or even feelings of inadequacy. Granted, this was based on the very little I have learned about you in our past several sessions, all of them disappointing. But gnawing questions remain on my part that leave me wholly dissatisfied with that, shall we call it, theory."

Snake leaned forward and said, "I always cry at weddings, especially my own. Did you watch the Dodgers on TV last night? Seven touchdowns!"

"However," the psychologist said, ignoring her comments, "Occam's Razor suggests something far more simple. The whole mess, the whole 'Snake' persona, is an act, a lie that you have fabricated not to escape your own demons, but to mask them and therefore to accomplish some inexplicable end."

Eacobacci leaned down and placed his hand on the cover of the magazine. It slid off the arm of the couch and fell to the floor. His face was only inches from hers.

"You are nothing but a common criminal, a fraud, a fake, a liar."

Unexpectedly, Snake grabbed his face in both her hands, and drawing him to her, kissed him with the mouth of her lipless Kabuki mask.

He jerked back and stood up, startled.

"Darling," she whispered through her Kabuki mask. "I think this is the start of a beautiful friendship. I'd gladly pay you Tuesday for a hamburger today."

The psychologist wiped his mouth with the back of his right hand.

What seemed like an hour but was really only twenty seconds crawled by without movement or sound from either the psychologist or Snake. He coughed his face stern and even flushing slightly red. His jaws were taut as he spoke.

"That was completely inappropriate.

"You are wanted by the police whom I suspect have only pretended to pursue you, considering the trouble you've saved them by nabbing the crooks you've left in your wake, and you are hunted by the local mob who want nothing more than to drink your blood as a toast. The bottom line is this. If you keep up this insane facade, I'm convinced you'll be dead within a month or so."

"Tut, tut tut. You don't know the half of it, lover boy," cooed Snake as she sat up from her reclining position. "Not even the half.

"I'm also a Nazi war criminal."

Carlos Valentine gingerly touched the tender flesh with the beefy index finger of his left hand around the cut closed by a butterfly bandage on his forehead just over his left eye. He hesitated before entering the recessed glass door to the shop. He would have given much to avoid the verbal beating or worse that waited for him inside.

To his immediate left and right were large, flyspecked, plate-glass windows full of a riot of dusty merchandise. A circular neon sign hung in the right window, blinking the words *DeSalvio 112*. Installed above the entrance was a window unit air conditioner that wept condensation, and above that, a sign that covered the entire length of the shop-front. It read:

112 John DeSalvio & Sons .... Co..Inc 112
DeSalvio'S GLASSWARE SUPPLIES
Wholesale & Retail BAR HOTEL and RESTAURANT Supplies On Display.

Carlos wore the meticulously pressed, pinstriped suit that had become his uniform in the Family. Even it looked too upper class for the dingy Bowery shop whose patrons were mostly the overweight, middle-aged, pot-bellied owners of the dives and narrow little bars that spotted skid row.

He plucked the *Lucky Strike* cigarette from his mouth with his right hand and flicked it away. The thug ran the same hand through his slicked back, black hair as he cringed at the thought of how Giovanni "The Hammer" DeSalvio would react to finally seeing his enforcer, the torpedo for the Family, only a handful of days after he had been beaten into submission by a woman in a crowded bar. He was certain his boss had heard of the incident. The humiliating news must have run like wildfire through the Bowery.

The thug shrugged his shoulders, sighed *what the Hell* in his head, shoved the glass door back, and stepped inside the neglected, poorly-lit store that was opened by Giovanni's father and the patriarch of the crime family, John DeSalvio, as one of his fronts and money-laundering operations before Carlos had even been born.

There was less than a handful of customers inside, all shirt-sleeve, working man types, milling around and looking at product, as Carlos began to search the long, narrow aisles for his boss. It took only a few moments to find Giovanni DeSalvio squatting in front of a bin pretending to be a clerk restocking light bulbs—a ploy that he continued although it had fooled no one who mattered for years except possibly his wife and children and a small number of casual friends outside the mob.

"Excuse me, sir," said Carlos. "I'm lookin' for them long, skinny light bulbs that you use in the ceiling to light a joint."

Giovanni looked up at Carlos as if he were staring at Elmer Fudd, but he looked, unflinching, at Carlos a little too long, until he finally said:

"You mean fluorescent bulbs, sir?"

Giovanni stood up. In general, he looked like a harried and un-groomed, middle-aged store clerk. He wore a white, short-sleeved shirt with a plastic protector holding several ink pens in its front pocket. His black, plastic belt was a little long, and his black slacks were somewhat shiny at the knees. His shoes were black, poorly polished, and cheap, and Giovanni's hair was brown, cut short, and crested with a substantial cowlick.

The head of the notorious crime syndicate, the DeSalvio Family, that ruled the underbelly of the Bowery with fists, bludgeons, and bullets, did not look like a caricatured Flattop, Mumbles, or the Brow from the *Dick Tracy* comic strip, nor did he resemble flesh and blood crooks like Al Capone, Dutch Schultze, or even Pretty Boy Floyd. He had no scar on his face, no torn ear, no broken nose, and didn't even look Italian. His only abnormality was a prosthetic, flesh colored, right hand clinched forever in a fist.

If hard pressed, Carlos would have said Giovanni looked like a handicapped Dagwood Bumstead. He just wouldn't have said it out loud.

"I'm certain we have exactly what you need, Mister," said Giovanni, "in the back room. If you'll just follow me...?"

As Carlos followed Giovanni back to the mouth of a narrow hallway leading away from the showroom, Giovanni said: "It's your lucky day. We're having a sell on fluorescent bulbs today."

Giovanni stepped to one side, and waved Carlos ahead of him with his left hand. As the DeSalvio torpedo passed him, the head of the crime syndicate slapped him too hard on the back with his prosthetic right hand in a false gesture of friendship for the sake of anyone who might be watching them from the showroom. Carlos clinched his teeth to suppress the pain.

Valentine said, "How's the wife and kids, Mr. DeSalvio?"

His voice dead, Giovanni answered, "They don't know you even exist, Carlos, and we're going to keep it that way. Right?"

"Yes, sir."

Under his breath and with a salesman's frozen smile, The Hammer added, "You have brought shame and humiliation to the family, Carlos. It would have been better if she'd killed you."

"But boss," Carlos began as they walked past dusty shelving full of restaurant supplies, "you don't know th' whole..."

"Shut up. This is the whole story. When I need someone squeezed, your job is to squeeze them until their eyes pop out. When I need a bone broken, you break it. When I need someone to stop breathing, you make them stop breathing. They should pee their pants when they just see you coming. Instead, a woman dressed like a circus clown beats the living Hell out of you and leaves you for dead in a crowded bar. Now they pee themselves from laughing at you.

"Here is the whole story. You need a cement bath because you stink."

As they neared an open door to their left, Giovanni shoved Carlos forward making him stumble.

"Get inside, dumb ass."

Carlos swallowed hard and went inside the open doorway.

Inside Giovanni's non-descript office, he watched the mob boss walk around a scarred, wooden desk piled high with stacks of papers, several magazines, and a half-folded newspaper, and sit in the desk's chair. Then and only then did he sit in a chair facing DeSalvio. The mob boss rocked back and forth in his chair for a while, his left hand clutching his right as his elbows rested on his knees. DeSalvio looked at anything but his henchman. Carlos felt a thin trickle of sweat crawl down the back of his neck to disappear under his shirt collar. Giovanni shook his head in disbelief.

"A woman," he muttered, and looked at Carlos. "A nutcase. Not only a woman, but some skirt who's been fouling up some of our business and costing me money."

"She's not just a woman, boss. She's a devil. If you'd seen her..."

"Shut up!" Giovanni yelled, and, snatching up the newspaper from his desk with his left hand, threw it at Valentine. "I have seen her! Everybody's seen her! Don't you read the newspapers, you illiterate moron!"

Carlos gingerly picked up the newspaper. On the upper fold of the *Zhurnal* was a headline that shouted "Exclusive! Photo of Bowery Mystery Vigilante!" The byline was Leo Rosenbaum's. The black and white photograph next to it was of Snake. Carlos looked up from the newspaper.

"Now I understand," said Giovanni, "why my father forced me to go to college." The muscles in his jaw were working and his expression was grim. "Here is what will now happen. You will follow my instructions step by step. You will find her. Then, when I have everything I want from this crazy skirt, you will kill her."

"But, Mr. DeSalvio, no one knows anything about her! Who she is. Where she lives. Nuthin'."

"You idiot, its right there in the newspaper."

Carlos reluctantly looked again at the lead news story and photograph of Snake. He looked at Giovanni, grinned his ignorance sheepishly, and shrugged his shoulders.

"You idiot. Who wrote the story?"

Carlos looked at the newspaper, and read the byline out loud.

"Leo Rosenbaum."

"Well?" asked Giovanni. "Well?!"

Carlos looked at the newspaper again, then at the mob boss, and shrugged again.

Giovanni slammed his prosthetic right hand down hard on the desk top. He leaned across the desk, his face flushed with anger, his eyes squinted.

"You poor, pathetic idiot.

"Find Leo," said Giovanni, "and you find Snake."

Leo Rosenbaum sat hunched forward in his good, heavy coat and his best Fedora in an army surplus, canvas folding chair with his forearms resting on the ledge of the building's roof as he watched the sun slowly rise in the East above the shorter buildings of the Bowery. A pair of high-powered, black binoculars rested on the ledge within his reach. His eyes were heavy from lack of sleep, his chin was stubbled and his face bore deep lines of disappointment. He could see the brief, pale condensation of his breath when he exhaled.

He had been watching the back of the Bowery Savings Bank at 130 Bowery across the alley that separated Bowery Street from the rear walls of the buildings on Elizabeth Street since midnight. It had been a cold and long night with a clear sky, but his camera that was mounted on its tripod to his right had not taken one photograph during the grueling stakeout.

To the right of the camera, Snake paced slowly along the ledge of the roof in full leathers, her blacksnake whip on her left hip, and her snake-headed quarterstaff balanced in her right hand. No matter the direction she paced, her attention never left the alley below them and the back of the bank. No one had been seen for hours except for a drunk covered with newspapers and sleeping at the mouth of the alley. Even during the long stretches of dead silence, she seemed to illogically make no sound as she walked away from the camera to the end of the building and then back to the tripod in an endless and hopeless loop.

For some time, Leo had been trying to break the monotony, the tension, and the silence in vain with an uninvited and ignored monologue about his life. Her indifference had not faltered.

"Just out of college," he began again, "I couldn't get a job at any of the major papers. So I sold advertising for a little publication, and wrote some features for them on the side. If it was just luck or the hand of God, I don't know, but after doing that for about four years, a job at the *Zhurnal* I managed to land.

"Say, if I'm boring you, just say so, and I'll jump off the ledge and we'll be done with this."

Snake said nothing.

"It would be better than nothing even to hear one of your strings of irritating quotes, you know."

There was no response.

"No, wait a minute, I've got it. Harpo Marx you are tonight. I'll be Groucho. If I complimented your beautiful body, would you hold it against me?"

There was no response.

"That was my Groucho Marx." Leo straightened in his chair and then stood up.

"The lady's got no sense of humor. Okay, I get it. My sources were bad or something and I've screwed up and wasted your time and my time and reputation. The DeSalvio thugs aren't going to rob the bank tonight.

"Listen, if don't get advanced stuff like this all the time, and my information seemed rock solid. I don't know what happened. Okay? If you know something I don't know, spill."

Snake stopped at the far side of the building and picked up a Walkie-Talkie on the ledge that had gone unnoticed by the reporter. She spoke several words into it, then stuffed the short-range mobile telephone in the waistband of her leather pants. She moved to the ledge and pointed down into the alley.

"Look," she said. "If you have nothing to say, say nothing. Look."

Leo watched as the bum lying at the mouth of the alley pushed the newspapers off of his body, stood up, and walked away. Simultaneously, the viper called Ham stood up from behind a group of trashcans and began to walk to the opposite end of the alley.

"Damn," Leo whispered. "What's going on here?"

"Adam was the luckiest man; he had no mother-in-law," Snake said. She added, "We're screwed. DeSalvio knows."

Chapter Eight

November 1944, Berlin, Germany

Berlin was dying.

Greta felt it was more than appropriate—it was ironic—to disguise herself as a widow in mourning as she stood in front of her chest-of-drawers wearing a long-sleeved black dress and shoes with a black pill-box hat secured to her hair with whale-bone pins. The hat's black veil was pushed up away from her pale, somber face and over the top of her hat.

Despite the formal attire for a funeral, Greta looked a little ungroomed; several strands of her hair were uncharacteristically wild, her makeup seemed half and hurriedly applied, and her general appearance was as if a once proud woman had made the best of a very a meager supply of cosmetics, powders, perfumes and toiletries.

The Nazi spy gently touched the outer edge of the framed photograph on the chest-of-drawers of herself and her dead sister—all pony tails, ribbons, and smiles. She kissed the black gloved index and middle fingers of her right hand, touched the image of her sister with the pads of those fingers, then laid the photograph face-down.

On the wall behind the chest-of-drawers were her four, treasured porcelain masks—a precious gift from one of the principal Nazi liaisons with the Japanese. He had also been her lover while he was alive. She carefully removed the rarest and most valuable of the four from its mountings, the white Kabuki mask of indifference, and carried it away with her to her couch.

For a moment and with a wistful smile, Greta watched her tortoise-shelled cat, Dolly, tumbling around next to her large, open, shoulder bag, playing with a partially unraveled ball of white twine. Greta sat down between the piece of luggage and the black and brown mottled cat, placed the Kabuki mask with some effort in the tightly-packed bag, and zipped it shut.

"Silly Billy," she said to the cat then playfully snatched the ball of twine away from Dolly.

Theirs was a delightful and long rehearsed ballet for the possession of the virtually worthless twine—a dance of playful lunges, gentle tugs, rapid-fire bites and attempts to clutch string with jaws and paws poorly designed to do so—until, as suddenly as it had begun, Dolly tired of the frustrating game, strutted disdainfully to the far end of the couch with her tail twitching, sat down, and began to clean her fore claws.

Greta noticed that the curtains for the apartment's one window were open, so she rose from the couch to close them. But her hands remained on the opened window-covering as she caught sight of two young boys playing in what once had been a park next door to her apartment complex.

They fought with sticks fallen from a tree next to a crater blown out of the ground by an Allied bomb. They fought valiantly and to the death in clothes that once would have only been worn by bums.

She closed the curtains and turned her attention back to her small and once lavish living room. Her best winter coat hung on a hook on the left side of the front door and over two small valises she had placed there earlier. Her jewels had been meticulously sewn beneath the lining of the coat.

Greta walked to Dolly's bowl, water dish, and bag of food sitting on the floor and next to the interior wall on the north side of her apartment. The water dish was already full to its lip. She opened the bag and filled Dolly's bowl with food. Then she closed the bag, tore open one of its sides, and left it gaping open on the floor.

The Nazi spy returned to the couch, picked up her shoulder bag and carried it with her to her front door. Greta then pulled on her coat, slung the strap of her bag over her shoulder, and opened the door. She stood in the doorway for what seemed to her to be at least an hour watching Dolly eat, taking a final inventory of the past several years of her life in the apartment. It was less than sixty seconds. Then she picked up her two valises, turned, and walked out of her apartment. She left the front door open.

When she reached the bottom of the stairs that lead to the main entrance and exit to her apartment building, she stopped, put down her two valises, and covered her face with her veil. She picked up her valises, adjusted her shoulder-bag, pushed the door open, and stepped onto the sidewalk.

With certain and reasonable strides, walking neither too fast nor too slow in fear she might draw attention to herself, she walked away from her apartment building.

She did not stop until she had left the city behind her.

Greta never saw Berlin again.

September 1952, Bowery, New York City

Armed only with his service revolver in its holster on his hip, his billy club in his right hand, and untested self-confidence in himself—after all, he'd been three weeks on the graveyard shift already— Jason Aldridge sang quietly as he strode east down a Bowery sidewalk in the middle of the night in the direction of Chatham Square. The residents of Gotham's most notorious stretch of businesses were obviously mostly asleep, all of the curious tourists had left the Bowery and traveled in their buses back to their hotels, and even the drunken bums had thrown in their alcohol soaked towels and called it a night. The street was empty of traffic, human and mechanical, its black stretch of concrete occasionally dotted with fuzzy-edged pools of yellow light cast from rare street lamps on the sidewalks.

As the rookie policeman moved to and through one of the yellow pools of light thrown down from a lamp onto the sidewalk, he reminded himself that his principle duty was to make sure the doors to the businesses were locked, so he stopped and dutifully rattled a doorknob. As he did so, Jason was reminded that his unspoken secondary duty was to endure the smell of beer and urine that seemed to permeate even the bricks of the now mostly dark and silent bars and dives that littered skid row. It wasn't particularly his favorite task. After all, he'd grown up in a respectable neighborhood in the Bronx.

He sang at two o'clock in the morning because, although he was the shortest cop in his precinct at 5' 6", he had graduated from the police academy at the head of his class and as the best shot of any boy or man of them. Early in the night, he had had no trouble rapping his billy club on a wall to wake up a drunken derelict and shoo him off of the street, and Jason knew he could handle any situation from a bank robbery to a gangland murder. So he pushed his cap back rakishly, revealing his jet-black, short-cropped hair, swaggered a bit, and sang George M. Cohen's "It's A Grand Old Flag":

♪You're a grand old flag,

You're a high flying flag ♩

And forever in peace may you wave.

You're the emblem of ♪ the land I love.

The home of the free and the brave.

♪ Ev'ry heart beats true 'neath the red, white and blue, where there's never a boast or brag..."

It was because Jason couldn't remember the rest of the lyrics that he finally heard the faint noises that his singing had obscured. The noises seemed to come from behind *Wooley's Fruits and Vegetables.*

His heart began to race as Jason turned off of the sidewalk to trot down the narrow space that separated the vegetable shop from its neighbor, his hand over the revolver in its holster. But the going was slow; there were no light posts—the alley was very dark—and it was cluttered with boxes and discarded furnishings, trash cans, and loose refuse.

Jason knew he should find a police call box and call for backup. But he didn't.

It was only his first mistake.

As the rookie neared the end of the dividing space that opened onto the alley behind the fruit and vegetable shop, the noise had become distinctly threatening, so he pulled his revolver and held it rigidly against his left thigh.

Behind him, Jack Frost wheeled silently out from behind a cluster of broken, wooden crates, his wooden oar lifted as if to strike. He hesitated, watching the receding cop's back as Jason entered the alley. Jack shook his head in disgust and growled to himself as if reluctantly obeying an order, then pushed himself back behind the crates.

Squatting down below the ledge that skirted the roof of a two story building that faced the space spilling into the alley, Leo Rosenbaum watched as Jason stumbled to a full stop in a pool of light. The reporter's camera was ignored; the lack of sufficient lighting made it useless now. His pen was poised over an open notebook.

But the pen never fell on the page; it all seemed to happen simultaneously. Jason raised his gun. In the dark, he saw the shadowy backs of four men moving away from him down the alley; it looked like the furthest one to his right was pulling a gun as he broke into a trot. One was carrying a large, black, leather valise. The back door to the shop hung broken on a single remaining hinge; additional light from the doorway spilled into the alley. In less time than it would take to even say it, the rookie cop realized they were advancing on what could only be a woman, one of her arms rigidly extended in front of her, although he could not be one hundred percent certain. She carried some kind of staff in her remaining hand.

Jason heard her say, "The only thing you have to fear...is me."

Jason broke into a trot as he barked, "Stop! Police!"

But the four burglars did not stop even as Jason heard a *thwip* and the thug pulling his gun dropped it, slapped the side of his neck, stumbled to his right, and fell face forward onto the concrete.

The distance separating Jason and the criminals was cut in half when the rookie again barked, "Stop! Police!" and leveled his gun as he ran. The three remaining burglars, ignoring his shouted warning and their fallen comrade, slowed as they neared the woman in leather. He guessed that they did not hear him. He could now see that the three thugs were facing a woman in a strange leather costume and mask.

Snake swung her extended right arm to target the thief at the left of the advancing trio. She said, "When you reach the end of your rope, tie a knot in it and hang on."

Jason did not own his second mistake that night. It was an Act of God.

The burglar targeted by Snake and directly in front of the rookie was one head taller than Jason. And as Snake pressed the dart pad in the palm of her hand, he ducked down and to his left side.

There was a *thwhit* sound.

Her dart whizzed over the shoulder of its intended target.

And buried itself in Jason's right eye.

It was all happening now at almost the same time.

The thug carrying the valise threw it at Snake. He missed.

Snake dropped her arm and snatched the blacksnake whip from her hip with her free hand. The whip snaked back over and to the right side of her shoulder, snapped forward, and wrapped its thong around the face of the thug to her right, drawing blood. He screamed and clutched at the bleeding whelp rising across his face as the thief who had ducked away from her dart began to run, plowed into and ricocheted off of Snake.

Leo rose from his hiding place on the roof and covered his mouth with his right hand, helpless to intervene.

He pulled his service revolver...

The thief who had thrown the valise ran full throttle for the mouth of the alley.

Jason fell down on the concrete alley road.

Snake rolled free of the glancing blow of the burglar who was now behind her, dropped her blacksnake whip, and tossed her quarterstaff from her left to her right hand. She swung one end of her quarterstaff up.

Ham, the bouncer, stepped into the mouth of the alley and in front of the burglar without the valise who had done an end run around Snake, his legs spread and anchored, his beefy hands on his hips.

As he sped past, Snake clubbed the thug who had tackled her on the back of his head with the end of her quarterstaff. He stumbled forward a few steps, trying but failing to maintain his balance and his consciousness, and fell, unmoving, near the mouth of the dark alley.

The rookie cop lay in the alley and did not move.

Ham smashed his raw-knuckled fist in the face of the last fleeing burglar. The thief fell like a clubbed ox.

Snake ran back to the body of the rookie cop. His blue cap, gun, and Billie club were scattered around him. Kneeling, she placed two fingers on the side of his neck.

She looked up through her inflexible Kabuki mask with a cobra coiled around her left eye down her cheek to the tip of her chin, her eyes behind it welling with tears. She did not move.

Overlooking it all, Leo whispered, "Mother of God."

The entire horrible farce had only taken seventeen seconds.

March 1945, Sachsenhausen, Germany

As the Nazi transport vehicle rumbled up to the entrance to the concentration camp, Max Riegelmann looked out through its glassless, barred window at the words worked into the left panel of the iron gate. They read: Arbeit Mach Frel.

There was a guard tower with an 8mm Maxim machine gun, but Max knew nothing about guard towers or guns, so he ignored both.

In the distance beyond an extremely large, open area, he saw what looked like a towering smokestack and a huge building that must house equally enormous equipment needed in manufacturing and a long row of barracks, all indicating to Max that Sachsenhausen was a factory. The air blowing in through the window smelled...less than pleasant...and the sky outside was overcast with lumpy, gray clouds. Unmistakably, he noted again, it was a factory. Therefore, the motto made complete sense, and he read the words with indifference.

Chained to his bench as were a half a dozen other men in the Nazi wagon, each of the seven prisoners—smelly, crumpled humps of dirty, matted hair and beards, sallow skin, and sunken eyes and cheeks—knew that indifference was the proper response to almost anything when fear and hope had been beaten out of someone who expected to be slaughtered.

Max Riegelmann did not know the place was named Sachsenhausen or that it was the closest concentration camp to Berlin, about 35 km north of the city. In fact, he had no clue that almost 200,000 Jews, Gypsies, homosexuals, and other "undesirables" had passed through those same gates over some period of time of the Third Reich and that 50,000 human beings had been brutally tortured and murdered there. Neither had the surgeon heard that Sachsenhausen, initially used to imprison Nazi political opponents, was now a killing field of the Holocaust.

Max had not heard of Sachsenhausen's sisters, Arbeitsdorf or Oberer Kuhberg, because, although the vast majority of his peers did not think of doctors and surgeons as scientists, Max was indeed a scientist. And scientists who had also been bullied, insulted, ostracized, and abused in their aborted childhoods learned to live their socially isolated lives with a scientific, objective, detachment.

The reasons for Rosenbaum's detachment were varied. Even though he was a highly sought after surgeon to the Nazi elite, Max was not invited to parties. So he had never heard the rumors that the Nazi guards at Auschwitz and Belzec knocked his Jewish brothers, sisters, mothers, and fathers to the ground and viciously kicked them with heavy jackboots, smashed their teeth out, or cut off the women's breasts. He had not heard their screams or the silence of the lambs.

Likewise, men who are deformed by dwarfism like Max don't attend the theater to enjoy the local gossip of genteel society, so he had no idea that, at Hinzert and Bogdanovka, prisoners were lashed to posts as their naked flesh was torn off their backs with sticks wrapped in barbed wire— the flesh of men and women and children who had already been starved. Or that some were hung, or marched in long lines as human skeletons to highly efficient and cost effective gas chambers and crematoria.

If Max had known, he might have been moved to compassion or even action. But Max had been busy making unattractive Nazi wives and whores beautiful under his sterilized scalpel.

To his credit, when, eventually and much too late, Max had been told, first by his twin brother, Franz, and then by the men of the *Sieg* that the Nazis were cutting body parts off of living humans to see how long they would survive, that Nazi scientists were using saltwater and electricity to gauge the level of pain that could be endured by the human body, that Nazi death squads were defaming, degrading, unleashing hungry dogs, and dropping prisoners, face down, on piles of glass shards, Max was horribly sickened and outraged.

But when Max had faced endless torture himself, he was left with only two options, to retreat from the excruciating pain into insanity or back into scientific, objective detachment. Max chose the objective insulation from reality of scientific observation. He had stepped out of his body to watch his own torment.

So he sat, hunched over in misery and chained in the transport vehicle with the hope, no matter how illogical, that the Nazi's had let him live so that they could get further information out of his crippled body of other anti-Nazi plots.

He would never know the truth that, facing certain defeat, humiliation, and the collapse of the Third Reich, the bureaucrats in Berlin had simply let him slip through the cracks of a dying regime in a mountain of neglected and forgotten paperwork.

As the Nazi transport vehicle passed through the entrance to Sachsenhausen, a thin, metal plate in the back wall of the cab slid back on a glassless slit and a voice barked, "Wake up. We're here." The metal plate was slid closed.

Max thought of the words worked into the left panel of the iron gate behind them now. The words had read: *Arbeit Mach Frel.*

Work Makes You Free.

He had expected death, but they had sent him to a factory as forced labor.

So how bad could that be?

He looked down at his forearm resting on the rough cloth that covered his thigh. On it was branded the numbers 665.

One short of the number of man.

Who would have guessed Max thought *that Nazis had a sense of humor?*

Chapter Nine

September 1952, Bowery Police Headquarters, 9th Precinct

The first police detective who entered the interrogation room nodded.

"Hey, Amy, how's the kid?" he asked and smiled as he walked past the police dispatcher where she sat at her cubicle.

"Just fine, Wayne," she answered. "She's doing just fine. In fact, she started piano lessons this week."

To stop her hands from shaking, Amy Smith focused her attention back on the metal pot of hot coffee in her hands and began counting each of the fourteen items on the little desk that sat at the right side of the entrance to the interrogation room again—five white, ceramic coffee mugs turned upside down, a coffee creamer, a spoon nestled in a small bowl of sugar, five spoons, and a coaster to protect the top of the desk from the heat of the coffee pot. Her mind did strange things when it was threatened.

She sat the coffee pot down on the doily.

As the first cop sat in a chair and the second and third policemen entered with polite greetings for her, Amy tried to focus on the five chairs she had placed in the middle of the small, plain, sterile room usually used to grill suspects. Setting up rooms was not in her job description, but, then again, doing whatever the precinct commander asked was done without hesitation or question. She patted several loose strands of her bleached blonde hair back into submission as the precinct captain, Sam Manning, who was uncharacteristically carrying a rolled up newspaper in his right hand, and one final policeman entered the room.

As Manning moved to the front of the five seated detectives, he nodded at Amy and said, "Thank you for your help, Miss Smith. That will be all for now."

She nodded and said, "Yes sir," and closed the door behind her but did not leave. She waited for several moments to make certain that no one else was entering the hallway, then opened the lower two buttons of her blouse.

Her eyes never leaving the hallway, Amy carefully pulled the tubing of a stethoscope out of the opening in her blouse, placed its ear-tips in her ears, and its diaphragm on the surface of the door.

She heard Captain Manning pacing in front of his men.

"Gentlemen, we are here today because Officer Jason Aldridge is dead. We cannot and will not tolerate the murder of one of our own. I have picked you five men as our best and brightest to form an internal investigative unit that will bring his killer to justice.

"Officer Aldridge was killed in the line of duty as he was trying to stop a burglary in process. We apprehended three of the perpetrators soon after their failed attempt to rob *Wooley's Fruits and Vegetables*, but all three deny having seen Jason's murder.

"Then there is this," Manning said, raising his rolled up copy of the *Tog Morgen Zhurnal* in his right hand. "This piece of...garbage. One of their reporters named Leo Rosenbaum has written that Aldridge's death was an accident caused by the leather-clad she-devil he has labeled 'The Snake'. This isn't the first time she has broken up a robbery or crime in progress, but I intend it to be the last. Jason's death was an accident only after *I* say it was an accident.

"The autopsy by the medical examiner revealed that the dart that pierced Jason's eye and brain was coated with a chemical compound meant to paralyze, not to kill. Nevertheless, you are to treat our suspect as armed and extremely dangerous.

"At the end of this meeting, you will each receive a full report of all the information on Jason's death that we have been able to gather as of today. Memorize it. Today, it will become your 'Bible'.

"You will report only to me. There will be no mistakes that can be used to toss this out in a court on a technicality. You will dot very i and cross every t.

"This...mad woman...has killed one of our own. You know what the needs of justice are in this case," Manning said. He did not say what was simply understood but never openly acknowledged, that once a cop has been killed, there is no need for the killer to be brought in alive. "I know that none of us will rest until this outrage perpetrated on one of our own is rectified. That having been said; take no undue risks and get the job done. Are there any questions?"

One of the detectives said, "Almost nothing is known about this woman. Do you have any idea where we should start, sir?"

Manning unceremoniously unrolled the newspaper and held it open. Aldridge's death and the only published photograph of Snake from a previous edition was the *Zhurnal*'s lead story.

"You start with the man who apparently does know something about her. Work in rotation. I don't want this reporter to take a leak without my knowing about it. Eventually, he'll lead us to the Snake.

"Unless there is anything else, you are dismissed."

Amy jerked the diaphragm off of the door, pulled the ear-tips from her ears, and began to shove the stethoscope back under her blouse even as she began to tiptoe-trot down the hallway. She buttoned her blouse and reached an intersecting hallway, turning into it as she heard the door to the interrogation room open. She immediately slowed to a brisk pace.

Her stomach a tightly wound ball of rubber bands, Amy sat down at the little desk in her cubicle with its four small, index card file cabinets, four black phones (one was wall mounted), her desk calendar, and an accordion bracket that, like an extended arm ending in a fist, ended in a microphone that jutted only inches from her face.

She looked to her right and then to her left, and then to her right again before her left hand fell to the edge of her desk and she threw a toggle switch just under its edge with her left index finger.

She spoke into the accordion microphone.

"The copper pot is boiling over. Turn down the heat"

Then her left hand fell to the edge of her desk and she threw the toggle switch back to its original position.

The police dispatcher rose from her desk, walked to the ladies' restroom, and entered. After checking each of its stalls to make certain that the room was empty, Amy Smith vomited in the sink.

March 1945, Sachsenhausen, Germany

I n the dead of a black night weeping a slow drizzle of miserable, cold rain, Max's heart was throbbing in his throat.

Covered with a film of flop sweat and fear, he and two other wretches desperately tried to paint themselves onto the exterior wall of their barracks, as they watched the slow sweep of the huge spotlight mounted next to the 8mm Maxim machine gun on guard tower A, at the entrance to Sachsenhausen.

The spotlight wasn't powerful enough to illuminate all of the barrack huts or the huge, semi-circular roll-call area immediately behind the main entrance, the infirmary or kitchens or laundry, or most of the massive ovens where the Nazis baked human biscuits, or even much of the almost ten-foot high stone wall that formed the perimeter of the concentration camp. Between that wall and a second, lethal, electric fence was a strip of gravel where guards and a starving pack of Rottweilers patrolled Sachsenhausen, as the spotlight momentarily dispelled the black of night before it passed on. But its sweep did light the supply truck from Berlin, parked outside the "special" barracks where the women lived who were too beautiful to kill immediately, and therefore served as whores for the elite of Sachsenhausen until their desirability diminished. When the drivers of the supply truck occasionally smuggled in a delicacy for the Commandant and his cronies, and it was too late to drive back to Berlin anyway, they spent the night there. Some even slept.

The spotlight swept, and Max and the other filthy, starving, inmates with sunken eyes and cheeks, dirty hair and beards, unclean hands, and teeth, and toothpick bodies, said not a word. The tiniest sound would spell death, so their almost hopeless plan of escape was communicated with their trembling, paper-thin, mottled hands, as they watched the truck.

The delicacy the truck carried tonight for three do-or-die escapees was freedom.

The spotlight swept, and Max gestured.

As one, the three pealed off of the wall and, hunching down as low as equilibrium would allow, began to skitter like crabs in the wake of the spotlight across the space between their barracks and the truck. So intense was their focus that, initially...

They did not hear the first horrible sound like cold metal scrapped quick across sandpaper. Or the second horror. But they heard the third yelp and the fourth racketing growl and the fifth howl join the first until it became a hideous and undeniable cacophony of savage barking rushing down on them like a nightmarish symphony.

The Rottweilers swarmed over the three men, a ravenous hoard of slavering yellow teeth slashing, ripping, tearing cloth and flesh, gashing bloody wounds like razor cuts that flailing arms and kicking legs could not stop. The otherwise silent night was rent with screams and the eventual laughter of Nazi guards as they breathlessly jogged up to the unholy fray one by one. Forming a semi-circle around the bestial carnage until, one by one, arms and legs gave no more resistance and three men lay like bloody, limp sacks on the ground as the guards began to kick and pull the Rottweilers away from their kill.

The lights snapped on in the windows of the special barrack.

The front door swung open and back, slamming against the exterior wall, and one of the truck drivers, still trying to pull up his pants low around his hips, was framed by the yellow light behind him.

He said, "Was zur Name den Teuffel...?"

The piece of bloody meat that had been Max Riegelmann hung loose and forward from his bound arms where he had been tied onto the only chair in a room, otherwise empty of anything but three, angry, exhausted Nazis and one naked light bulb, hanging from the clapboard ceiling.

It was three o'clock in the morning.

"You are quite the brave idiot," snarled the Nazi standing in front of Max. "Your barracks, all of the barracks, are wired. We knew of your idiotic plan to escape long before you took the first step."

Max's head hung low over his chest. He said nothing.

Holding his pistol by its butt, the Nazi pistol-whipped Max across the side of his head. In a spray of spit from his mouth, the surgeon's head flopped away from the arc of the gun, and then back to its original position. Max didn't even grunt.

"Something almost unheard of for a Nazi, has apparently happened. It was believed that a little vacation to Sachsenhausen Resort would loosen you up a bit and we'd get to add to our list of traitors to the Fatherland. But we were wrong. A Nazi wrong. Imagine that."

The officer who had struck Max across the face turned to his two companions.

"Gentlemen," he said, "I believe the time has come…"

The Nazi gun-whipped Max again. In a spray of blood from his mouth, the surgeon's head flopped away from the arc of the gun, and then back to its original position on his chest. The Nazi leveled his gun against Max's right temple. One of the other soldiers looked up at the ceiling.

"…to finish what we thought the dogs would do, kill the worthless rat right now!"

The door behind the three Nazis swung open and back, slamming against the interior wall, and a fourth guard, almost out of breath, was framed by the room's yellow light. He held a piece of paper in his right hand. The Nazis torturing Max turned to face his fellows. They looked at one another and shrugged indecision with their shoulders.

The Nazi officer snarled, "How dare you interrupt an interrogation ordered by the Commandant himself!"

The guard in the doorway gasped, waving the piece of paper. His uniform was dirty and in disarray.

"An urgent message!" He sucked in air, trying to gain not only oxygen but his composure itself.

It was then that the three Nazis facing him realized that his expression promised something dire, horrible almost beyond comprehension.

"The Red Army is at…our doorstep. All of the prisoners, all of them, are to be evacuated, immediately."

The soldier held up the piece of paper and waved it in the air. "On the orders of Adolf Hitler himself."

The Nazi officer's pistol fell to the side of his right leg, forgotten.

Chapter Ten

April 27, 1945, Sachsenhausen, Germany

As the Russian medical vehicle from the 1st Belorussian Front of the Red Army of the Soviet Union lumbered through the main entrance to Sachsenhausen, its weary driver looked out one of the vehicle's windows at the words worked into the left panel of its iron gate. He could not read: Arbeit Mach Frel.

He looked back at his relief driver and said, "Here we go again."

The long trek from Oranienburg had been grueling for the already exhausted first wave of Russian and Polish soldiers. They had not been ordered from the front lines to liberate a concentration camp in what they instinctively knew were the last days of World War II. Burning hottest in their hearts was revenge for the millions of their brothers and sisters and children who had been murdered by the invading Nazis. Initially, none of them even knew of the 3,000 horrors, too sick and weak to have been evacuated, that had been left behind in Hitler's evacuation of Sachsenhausen. Nevertheless...

By the time the truck parked on the rutted road in front of the barrack, its driver and the odd assortment of Soviet and Polish medical personnel inside were sleep deprived and on the edge of emotional and physical collapse.

As they disembarked from the truck, they all wore surgical masks because they knew what awaited them now.

One of the medics said, "It smells like a slaughterhouse in here."

They worked their way methodically and carefully through the room full of fetid piles of rotting flesh that had once been men and women, stacked on a chaos of mostly wooden benches and tables, although some with arms and legs askew were thrown on the floor like crazy dead marionettes, as if someone had dropped what they had been doing as they fled. The carnage did not faze them. They had long been hardened against carnage by the horrors of war.

It was a Polish medic who placed the gloved pads of his index and middle fingers on the major artery of Max Riegelmann's neck, waited for the count, then shook his head in disappointment. He genuflected with his left hand before moving to the next corpse.

"Another one for the grave," he said more for the benefit of maintaining his own sanity by hearing his own voice than for the sake of the other men.

"Bastards," he added for the benefit of God's ears.

That's when the ghastly thing on the table that was Max Rieglemann jerked up, turned his head to his left side, and spat up blood.

He gurgled, "Gretchen."

September 1952, Bowery, New York City

I t was a beautiful, clear, and temperate day in Gotham. Leo Rosenbaum shifted his weight from his left to his right foot and surveyed the visual chaos of magazines and newspapers that filled *Michael McCormick's News Stand* at 99-101 Bowery Street. There wasn't a cloud in the sky, the air was crisp and clean, and the sounds of the traffic on the street behind him were so familiar that they were negligible as he stood, a bit overheated, in the overcoat that his wife, Annabel, had forced him to wear before he left for the *Tog Morgen Zhurnal* offices. The reporter read the masts of the magazines as he whistled Doris Day's "A Guy is a Guy". It was just a work day like any other work day in his life.

To his right side stood a man dressed in a nondescript suit with his face hidden by his opened copy of the *New York Times* as a thin swirl of smoke rose above the newspaper to dissipate in the air. Leo noticed that the lead story in the *Times* was the latest news about President Dwight Eisenhower.

As he scanned the periodicals, the *Zhurnal* reporter was a man perpetually torn between two loves. His first passion was the organized forest of multi-colored paper on the shelves of the newsstand that was his first, secret desire—slick magazines like *The Saturday Evening Post, Look,* and *The Atlantic Monthly* that all paid high rates for fiction. Displayed among these were the lower paying and garish pulps, among them *Dime Detective Magazine, Max Brand's Western Magazine, Weird Tales, Marvel Science, The Shadow,* and *Amazing Stories.* Above these and strung like laundry on a wire were the relatively new comic book magazines that were scraping the bottom of the barrel for any aspiring writer—*Forbidden Worlds, Superman, Battlefront, Planet Comics, Captain Marvel Adventures* and *Howdy Doody.* He knew that he'd probably be adding rejection letters from them to his growing pile of disappointments before long.

Interrupting the reporter's reverie, the newsstand owner handed him what Leo actually bought each work day, a copy of the *New York Times*.

"Mornin', Mr. Rosenbaum," said McCormick. "Made that first big sell yet?"

"Nah, just another form letter last week. This one from *Collier's*. A break I can't seem to get."

"They just don't know talent when they see it, Mr. Rosenbaum. I loved that one you let me read about the cannibal and the mermaid. Count your blessings. At least you have your job at the *Zhurnal*."

"At least," said Leo as he smiled apologetically and meekly handed McCormick a dime. "At the very least."

Behind the newsstand stood the reporter's second love, a piece of Bowery history, the building that once housed *Worth's Museum and Congress of Living and Inanimate Curiosities*. The dime museum, which Leo had never actually visited when it was in business, had been opened by E. M Worth in 1881 and held a special place in Leo's heart because of his attraction to the spectacular and lurid. *Worth's* had once offered up spectacular living and inanimate oddities, many of them frauds, to city-bound crowds hungry to escape the mundane world. For decades, their dimes had won the gape-mouthed, the gullible, and the very young a glimpse of a live, giant squid, or an elephant, rhinoceros, or giraffe—weird creatures indeed to the untraveled and unsophisticated lower classes of Gotham. *Worth's* also displayed the purported preserved head of Charles Julius Guiteau, the man who had assassinated President James A. Garfield, next to the mummified remains of a tiny Wolf Boy and Mermaid. And the beer sold there had been cold and cheap.

Some part of Leo still wished that he had been among the children who had bought a live mouse to feed the "giant" snakes in the museum's menagerie and won themselves free admission by doing so.

Rosenbaum sighed and shrugged his shoulders as he filed his two passions under "unrequited" then rolled up his newspaper and tucked it carefully under his left arm. He waved at McCormick as he left the newsstand, walking past the customer reading the *Times* without giving him so much as a second thought. As the reporter passed him, the *Times* was lowered, revealing the reader's face as he watched Leo's back diminish and then disappear among the people milling on the sidewalk.

It was the face of Hank the hack.

Lieutenant Manning stopped at Leo Rosenbaum's desk nestled among the five other battered and scuffed desks in two parallel rows of three desks each in the bullpen. The reporter, chewing on his pipe as he was typing, raised his left hand with a raised index finger, miming a request 'for a moment, please'. The sound of clacking typewriters reminded the policeman of rapid, random, and loud reports of multiple handguns being discharged at the Bowery police station's indoor firing range.

"I'm Lieutenant Manning of the ninth precinct, Mr. Rosenbaum, and I'm not usually asked to wait by people. And I don't react well to being blown off, either, so ditch that idea."

Leo raised his bare head and stopped typing.

"Lieutenant Manning, eh? A visit from the police I've been expecting for some time now. I must admit I'm surprised that they sent the top dog. What can I do for ya?"

"You can start by telling me everything you know about this character you've been calling the 'Snake', including where she parks her carcass."

Leo quickly looked around the room to see if any other reporter was paying attention to him or the lieutenant. No such luck.

"In private, Lieutenant. Please...?" Rosenbaum pushed his chair back from the desk and pointed at a closed door in the back wall of the bullpen.

"In there, Lieutenant." Said Rosenbaum as he stood up. "So why me? We aren't the only paper covering the exploits of that madwoman."

"You've got to be kidding," answered Manning as both approached the door to the conference room. "You published the only known photograph of her."

"Oh, yeah, that," faux grinned Leo as he opened the door to the room. "Yeah, that."

Rosenbaum pulled a chair back from the small table in the room and waved an invitation for the policeman to sit opposite him. Leo sat down as Manning pulled back a second chair and complied with the reporter's request.

"I'm sure you've heard of the law that says a reporter doesn't have to give up his sources, lieutenant, so this is probably going to be a waste of your time and mine. I'm on a deadline, so..."

"And I'm equally sure you know I've heard that old canard about a thousand times before today. But today is special. A cop is dead."

"An accident it was. I can get you a copy of our edition of my story—it was the lead—if you missed it."

"Really," said Manning, "and just how do you know it was an accident?"

"From one of the thugs who Snake interrupted when they were robbing a joint that you guys arrested after the fact. I interviewed him at your precinct, which you'd already know if you were on top of things."

There was fire burning in the lieutenants eyes now.

"I did know, smart ass. And you passed the test."

"Good," said Leo, rising from his chair. "Very good. You can send my diploma in care of this newspaper. I'll hang it right next to the gold star I got in high school for learning my civic responsibilities."

"Apparently, you were sick the day they taught respect for policemen. But before you trot back on your high horse to fairyland, Mr. Rosenbaum, I've got a question I'd like you to answer. What's more important, the life of the next person that she'll kill or the public's right to know?"

"The trick answer to your quick question," said Leo, sitting down again, "is that both are equally important. So maybe there won't be a next time if I do my job and you do your job and then we'll both dance our way down the yellow brick road to fairyland together, hand in hand. So, unless you'd like to buy a subscription while you're here—and I think you'd benefit from that—I think we are done dancing. Do you think you can find your way out by yourself, Lieutenant Manning?"

"I'm really good at finding things," snarled Manning as he began to rise. "So you keep your precious, imaginary, power-of-the-press, and I'll do what I do best. You should know that every step you take from now until the Snake is arrested will be watched, Mr. Rosenbaum. For your own protection, of course. You won't be able to take a leak without my knowing it."

"Good to know," said Leo, standing up as well, "you're a pervert as well as a cop. Now, good day, lieutenant."

Leo left the *Tog Morgan Zhurnal* bullpen and its scuffed desks and the front pages of newspapers simply thumb tacked to the walls and a calendar or two by the clock that read 4:54pm. He walked down the hallway past the sign above the door that read "City Editor" and above the second sign that read "Managing Editor" to the stairs that descended to the classified advertising department of the newspaper.

The doorbell chimed at 4:54pm, and Annabel Rosenbaum closed the pasteboard covers of her husband's unpublished novel, a work-in-progress he'd titled *Westchester Weekend*, laid it on the small end-table next to Leo's favorite chair, and stood up.

She patted her hair back into place as she walked to the front door to their apartment. She knew it couldn't possibly be Leo; it was too early. She composed the little speech she'd use to dismiss whatever salesman would

"...you can find your way out...Lieutenant..."

greet her, and opened the door.

"May I help you?" asked Mrs. Rosenbaum as she stood smiling in the doorway.

"You bitch," said Carlos Valentine.

Leo descended the stairs whistling Kay Starr's "Wheel of Fortune" and gloating that he had routed Lieutenant Manning. Of what little he had accomplished of his dreams for himself at this point in his life, the reporter was extremely proud that he did wield the pen that was mightier than the sword—the police in this instance, and he wore his pride like a medal.

Carlos Valentine shoved Annabel back from the open door using palms of his open hands and his arms like a battering ram. She gasped as he shoved her, clutched her chest with both hands where Carlos had pushed her, and stumbled back, her expression turning almost instantly from surprise to terror as Carlos with rat-faced "Knife" Randuzzi close behind followed her backwards dance into her apartment.

At the foot of the stairwell, Leo found himself facing the long desk and the neatly but modestly dressed young woman sitting behind the desk in charge of classified advertising. She was a pleasant and welcome part of his daily routine, but she did not initially realize he was standing there. It was 5:01pm.

"You know what to do," said Carlos as he split away from "Knife," who followed Annabel's backwards retreat as she partially regained her footing. The blood drained from her face, and with her eyes wide with horror, Annabel made a futile attempt to protect herself from Randuzzi by raising a forearm. But he was on her in a split second and jerked her forearm down. Carlos walked to Leo's chair

The Hammer's thug picked up Leo's manuscript, opened it, and tore it in half at the spine. He let it drop to the floor as he swept everything off of the end-table with his left forearm. The lamp, the ashtray, and the half-empty glass of water that Annabel had been drinking smashed as they fell to the floor.

"Knife" raised his right arm across his chest and backhand-slapped Annabel across the face. Tears welled in her eyes as she chocked and stumbled back hard against a wall and raised her forearm across her face again. Sneering, "Knife" Randuzzi backhanded-slapped her across the face again, and said:

"I likes me women, Valentine." It was 5:01pm.

"Shut up!" Carlos barked and began tearing framed artwork and photographs off of a wall and throwing them over his shoulder. "You ain't doin' that now. Remember what the boss said. Nothing permanent."

"Yeah, yeah, yeah," "Knife" answered and forehand-slapped Annabel, who was whimpering, across her now blood-flushed face.

"Good evening, Mr. Rosenbaum," said the classified sales lady and receptionist with a perfunctory smile. "All in for today? Give my regards to the Mrs."

"See you tomorrow, Rosie," Leo answered. It was 5:03pm.

His own blood now pounding in his veins, Carlos began to overturn furniture, tossing each small piece behind him like trash, as his own adrenalin began to boil into fury as he moved around the apartment.

Careful to restrain in own animal savagery, "Knife" brought his knee up into Annabel's stomach, and she slid down the wall, sobbing.

She tried to say Leo's name, but could not speak. It was 5:03pm.

The *Zhurnal's* star reporter paused behind the glass door recessed between two large, plate glass windows displaying assorted, inexpensive, watches, bracelets, and trays of rings and necklaces. He made a mental note for himself that he really should buy a nice bracelet or necklace for Annabel someday. Leo could almost smell the baked halibut with almonds waiting for him at home. It was 5:06 pm.

At 5:06pm, "Knife" Randuzzi punched Annabel in the face, splitting her upper lip and breaking one of her front teeth. Carlos Valentine stopped his rampage through Leo and Annabel's living room, and turned back to face Randuzzi.

"That's enough, rat-face," said Valentine.

"Don't...call...me...Ratface," said Randuzzi, and began choking Annabel.

Because the reporter could read Hebrew, Leo absentmindedly glanced at the backwards lettering there as he did every day that translated said "The Morning Journal", shrugged his slight shoulders, pushed the door open, and left the building.

The sidewalk was crowded with workers leaving for home, shop keepers closing up their businesses, and bars preparing for a crowd, but he stepped into the flow of the milieu without hesitation and was soon carried away in its current. It was 5:07 pm.

"I said that was enough!" Valentine barked as he stood behind "Knife" who was crouching over Annabel sitting on the floor, shaking her as he choked her.

"Knife" continued to choke her.

Carlos grabbed him from behind under his armpits and pulled him off of Annabel. Randuzzi's breathing was labored, his expression was blank, his eyes unfocused and mad. Carlos slapped him. Hard. "Knife" shook his head as if he were awakened from a nightmare. He was. It was 5:08pm.

Leo walked briskly and life was all business as usual and the reporter never noticed the man reading a newspaper as he leaned against the corner of a building.

Carlos stood over Annabel who was sobbing on the floor and clutching her stomach as three cuts in her forehead bled tiny rivulets of blood down her pale face, one joining the pool of blood at the left corner of her mouth.

"Believe it or not, it's your lucky day, sister," the thug sneered as "Knife" stood behind him trying to catch his breath. "I could have let Knife, there, have his way with you. But it's not about you today."

Carlos dropped a folded piece of paper on her lap where the folds of her dress had formed a concave depression.

"That's for Leo," added Carlos. "He'll explain everything." And so saying, Valentine, with Randuzzi immediately behind him walked to and out the open doorway to Leo and Annabel Rosenbaum's apartment. Although it didn't register with Annabel, she heard the two men stop outside of the door.

Carlos said, "Close the door. What are you, a slob?"

She heard the door close. It was 5:10pm.

It was 5:10 pm. As Rosenbaum passed the man leaning against the wall, he lowered his copy of the *New York Times* and watched the back of the reporter until Leo was almost completely swallowed up by the crowd. Then he jerked away from the wall, folding his newspaper. With deliberation, he melted quickly into the crowd, following the reporter.

It was Ben Aleshee.

It was 5:21 pm. Leo stood as if felled by an ax in the doorway of his apartment, his eyes welling with terror and tears, and whispered: "Anna?"

He was at her side where she lay on the floor in a breath. Kneeling, he cradled her bruised head in his arm and brushed her hair out of the rivulets of blood that now crawled down her face, over her jaw, and down her neck. She was barely conscious and whimpering when her eyes fluttered.

Leo said, over and over, "oh god, oh god, oh god, oh god. Who did this to you?"

Unable to speak, Annabel picked up the folded paper from her lap and held it up in Leo's line of vision. He took the paper, opened it and read the typewritten message.

Annabel straightened up from his chest just an inch, and whispered with her split lip and through her broken tooth:

"What...does...it mean?"

The note read: Snake or Annabel.

No cops

We'll be in touch.

It was then that the reporter heard the voice that refocused him from the message of the note to the doorway of his apartment.

That voice said, "Is she okay?"

The woman in the doorway was built like a wooden beer keg dressed in a floral shift. Her brown hair was cut short like a man's, her lips were ruby red, her cheeks were heavily roughed, and her bared, uneven teeth were brown from tobacco stains.

"Where the Hell were you!" Leo managed to say. "You were supposed to protect us, dammit!"

"We were told to follow you," said Typhoid Mary, "not your wife. We made a mistake. But there's no time for this.

"Pack a bag. Annabel's goin' on vacation."

September 1945, Somewhere in Europe

The haggard old man who looked to be in his late seventies sat down heavily behind his maple desk stacked with loose papers and sighed. He was one of the answers to what to do with Nazi Germany after the Allied victory had been discussed in all of the meetings between Stalin, Franklin Roosevelt and Churchill in Casablanca, Teheran and Yalta. The big dollops of human flesh that lay like candle wax under his eyes were a silent testament to the endless hours of heated debate and concessions that had created the war crimes tribunals held under the authority of the Allied powers.

The old man took off a heavy pair of black-rimmed glasses, and began to wipe them clean with a handkerchief removed from the suit pocket over his left breast.

"Please," he asked of the tall, thin man standing on the opposite side of the desk, "sit down."

The tribunals had been free to do as they wished because Germany had surrendered unconditionally. The International War Crimes Tribunal had sat under the authority of the USSR, Great Britain and the United States with France added late to the proceedings. But the most well remembered tribunal would be at Nuremberg on November 20th, 1945 and would not conclude until October of 1946 as the most prominent political and military leaders of the Nazis were tried for war crimes.

But there was more to the process than was publicized, and the old man was part of that more as was the man who now sat uneasily across the desk from him.

Ben Alashee sat down, took a Camel cigarette from his shirt pocket, removed a Zippo lighter from the left pocket of his trousers, and lit the cigarette. He placed the Zippo on the edge of the desk.

He was in his forties, bald, wore several days of stubble on his chin, and had the prominent nose most associated, rightly or wrongly, with a Semitic heritage. His clothing was nondescript. He was known as Ben Alashee, although that was not his name, and he sat at the desk because if the axiom that it takes a thief to catch a thief is true, then it takes a spy to catch a spy must be true as well. Ben had been a very successful spy assigned to the British during the war, and was now semi-unemployed.

The old man tossed a folder across the desk to Ben, who picked it up and began to look through it as his potential employer began to talk.

Alashee slowly removed his Camel from his mouth and blew a slow stream of smoke into the air.

"This one was one of the worst, Mr. Alashee, as you will see very quickly as you review the file. Most of the information was given up by a Colonel Wolfgang of the SS when he was captured as part of a plea bargain for his life. This operative of the now defunct Brillenschlange that led so many freedom fighters to their deaths is now officially a Nazi War Criminal and must be caught, dead or alive. But she seems to have fallen off of the face of the earth just before the fall of Berlin."

Ben stuck his Camel back into his mouth to talk around it.

"I believe there isn't a picture in the file," said Alashee. "Do you know what she even looks like?"

The old man threw an 8"x10" photograph across the desk.

"One of her names was Gretchen Hoffmeyer. That's a publicity shot from one of the last movies she made before the commercial film industry had fallen into silence in Germany, It was called *Was in Himmel?* and she was little better than a bit player in it and the other small budget films that she initially used as her cover. Don't think for a minute that because they were cheap films that she wasn't and isn't a consummate actress. She was able to fool a baker's dozen of highly placed men to the extent that they betrayed their families and their nations and spilled their guts.

"We are certain that she is no longer in Germany, but we have no idea if she is even still in Europe. She may be trying to leave the continent for America, and she has the resources to do so. She is a very rich woman. Many rich men gave her very expensive gifts in exchange for, let us call them, special favors."

Alashee studied the photograph for a moment as the not so distant memories of the North African Campaign in 1940 that had been fought in the Libyan and Egyptian deserts and in Morocco, Algeria, and Tunisia flashed through his mind. Those memories started with the declaration of war by Italy on June 10, intensified by June 14 when the British Army's 11th Hussars crossed the border from Egypt into Libya and captured the Italian Fort Capuzzo, and ended for Ben in the bloodbath at Sidi Barrani in September, that left the bloody bodies of his mother, father, sister and her family in the desert sands. He tossed the photograph back on the desk.

"She *is* drop-dead gorgeous. If she's fallen off of the face of the earth, then I'll need a space ship to find her." He removed his cigarette and blew smoke.

"You'll be given all of the resources you'll need to find and apprehend her."

"Apprehend?"

"This is not a dead or alive situation. Apprehend."

"How long do I have to find this Gretchen Hoffmeyer?"

The old man grinned. Alashee stuck his cigarette back in his mouth.

"Until Hell freezes over or she is in it."

September 1952, Bowery, New York City

The woman was naked.

She walked down the hallway without shame or humility with her left arm laced in the right arm of the doctor that had just bandaged Annabel's wounds and abrasions and given her a sedative.

Annabel closed the door that she'd opened a crack in an effort to leave, and back-stepped into the room where a woman, who also looked like a man and a younger woman in a simple white blouse and black trousers watched her; both sat in chairs next to a large bed. There was no other chair in the room, so Annabel returned to the bed and sat down.

"Changed your mind on leaving, eh?" commented the manly woman.

"This...this is a...whore house," Annabel said, with her head somewhat lowered.

"Bingo," answered the lumberjack of a woman around the cigarette hanging from the corner of her mouth. "I was going to call it the 'Palace of Unimaginary Delights' but they charge by the letter when they paint signs, and cops arrest you for false advertising.

"They calls me Typhoid Mary, and this is my whore house, and this here is my daughter, Amy Louise Smith. I'm an operative of the Snake, so is Amy, and now you know that Leo is the newest member of our little nest of vipers. Sooner or later that will all sink in, and you'll understand that what your hubby did in sending you here was a good thing. We watch each others' backs."

Amy leaned forward in her chair. "Are you feeling any better, dear?"

"Yes," she responded as she chewed a fingernail on her left hand. "A little. What do you mean by an 'operative'?"

"Well, most people don't think about it but the cops mostly clean-up after crimes, but Snake wants to stop 'em from happening. So we act as her eyes and ears, picking up info on where something's gonna happen before it happens so she can stop it. You know. Operatives. The girls pick up tips from the johns that I pass on, and Amy is a police dispatcher. Hank, the cabbie that brought us here, is a one of us, and he keeps his ears wide open all the time. There are others, my ex-husband, as example. And we all pass on the information to Snake. And I guess you're also an honorary one now because of Leo. Sorta by association, I guess."

Annabel looked around at the room in her best attempt to not look at the two women with her. The wallpaper was flowered, there was a small vase of fresh flowers sitting on a doily on the night table standing next to the large bed against the wall and in the center of the room, and two, oc-cupied large chairs. The room smelled clean and fresh as well. The bed was neatly made up with a comforter and extra throw-pillows randomly lean-ing against two overstuffed pillows at its headboard.

It looked like a respectable woman's bedroom, but Annabel was rapidly learning not to accept appearances on face value anymore.

"Amy is your daughter?" she asked in an attempt at normal conversation.

"Last time I checked," said Typhoid. "Oh, I get it. No, Amy isn't a pros-titute. Most of what I did in opening my little house was so that she'd nev-er have to follow in my footsteps. Your second unspoken question: does she approve of what her momma does. Hell no. That was most of the rea-son why she left when she found it out as a teenager. Then she got herself in her own problems. So she's grown up some since then and learned that a woman does what a woman has to do to keep a roof over her head, clothes on her back, and food on the table for her family."

Annabel looked at Amy who was obviously unhappy at the direction the conversation had taken and was squirming a bit in her chair.

"But Leo said this 'Snake' woman is a criminal because she keeps what she takes from the gangsters and that she's also a madwoman because of the way she dresses and that Kabuki mask."

"No offense, but don't believe everything you read in the papers, hon-ey" said Amy. "If you think that makes us criminals too, you're welcome to your opinion, I guess, but you'd be wrong. Mama started with her for the money, and told her about me who started out for the money as well. Single mother and all. But neither one of us does it just for the dough now. As for her being a madwoman, in my opinion, she's crazy like a fox."

"That's where Sugar Cookie and I disagree," said Typhoid.

"Mamma, please don't call me that."

"Sorry, honey," said Mary, then turned to Annabel. "When her own daughter gets a little older, Amy will understand why she'll always be my little Sugar Cookie. Sure, Snake is crazy. But after you've been around the block a couple of times, you figure out that everyone is a little crazy, just in different ways. And it's anybody's guess why she wears the Kabuki mask. The papers think it's because a jilted lover threw acid in her face, or that she was born butt-ugly—excuse my language—or that she does it to hide her true identity like one on the Mystery Men in the pulp magazines or the superheroes in the comic books. But the truth is, no one really knows.

"Why don't you ask her yourself?"

Then suddenly, illogically, she was there, in the room, standing behind Annabel on the opposite side of the bed.

Annabel covered her mouth with her right hand to stifle a gasp.

She was dressed in leather, her torso accented by a dark blue bustier held closed by draw strings. Leather flames of a slightly lighter blue that rose up from its bottom spread to and across her ribs. What looked like fish or snake scales were embossed in her bustier. Her long, brown hair fell in satin waves to the tops of her breasts, and the leather armlets that covered her wrists up her forearms were also laced closed. Her tights ended in boots that ended just above her calves.

In her left hand, she held a quarterstaff easily five feet long topped by a cobra's head. On her left hip was a coiled blacksnake whip.

Her face was hidden by an expressionless, almond smooth, Kabuki mask, with a hand-painted cobra on its left side.

Walking with pronounced energy around the bed to Annabel, Snake knelt by Leo's wife and raised a hand so gently, oh so gently, placing the fingertips of her left hand over one of Annabel's bandaged cuts without touching it.

"'If anyone causes one of these little ones," Snake said, "to stumble, it would be better for them if a large millstone were hung round their neck and they were thrown into the sea. Who did this to you, little kitten?"

"I heard one of them call the other one 'Knife,'" answered Annabel.

"'Knife' Randuzzi, a thug from the DeSalvio crime family. I can't say I'm surprised," Snake said. "It is my fault that you were hurt, little one, and I want you to know that just as I have been punished for the evil that I have brought into the world, these men shall be punished ten times over. There is nothing so annoying as to have two people talking when you're busy interrupting."

"What?" said Annabel.

"She goes off on a tangent sometimes," explained Amy. "Just stick with her."

"Is there anything else that you wish to know that Typhoid or Amy have not told you, little kitten?"

Now Annabel raised her right hand and gently placed its fingertips on the cold, hard, smooth almond cheek of Snake's Kabuki mask.

"Does it hurt?" she asked.

Chapter Eleven

May 1946, Berlin, Germany

Max Rieglemann stood next to his hospital bed in a very plain, cheap, blue suit with a small, cardboard suitcase at his feet as the Chief Surgeon of the austere unit handed him an envelope. His neatly made bed was one of twenty on the east side of the ward; randomly, about sixteen of them were occupied with wounded, crippled, or near death patients.

"It's $100 American. It isn't much," said the surgeon as he looked down at his clipboard, "but at least it will help get you back on your feet, Dr. Rieglemann."

The military surgeon looked up.

"Every thing checks out, health-wise. You've certainly gone through Hell, and you are lucky, to say the least, to even be alive. Every thing is working like it should—I don't have to explain that to you, of course—so count your blessings. I really encourage you not to ruin the rest of your life with bitterness over the past. I've seen too many men do just that. Forgive and forget is my best advice. If you can't forgive, at least forget."

"I can never repay you for what you've done for me, doctor" said Max and extended his right hand. The doctor took the offered hand, and they shook vigorously for a moment out of professional courtesy if not out of a sincere affection for one another. "I'm going to try my best to take your advice."

Max bent at the knees slightly and picked up the suitcase.

"Do you think you'll go back into practice?" asked the surgeon. "I know that wouldn't be easy, but this war ravaged country of yours desperately needs every doctor it can get. I might even be able to find the right contacts who would give you the initial funding you'll need to re-establish an office."

"The Allies blew up my building," said Max, "during the last bombings."

"Oh, I'm so...well, I guess I can't actually say I'm sorry. But it had to be done; it was your war, not ours. I know you never supported the Nazis; that much is in your favor."

"I was a coward," said Max.

There was an awkward, long moment of silence as the surgeon struggled to know what to say in response.

"I can't honestly say I wouldn't have taken the same path as you did if I'd had to face the Nazis. We are all cowards about some things. I'm afraid of spiders."

The surgeon smiled at his own weak attempt at whimsy.

"You can always open up another office in another building, of course."

"Possibly," said Max. "I don't really know. Maybe, but there are too many ugly memories here for me, doctor, too many horrors that I desperately want to forget. I have no family left here—they were all killed by the Third Reich. I never had many friends. No...girlfriends, either. So, if I do return to practice, it won't be in Germany."

"I am sincerely sorry to hear that, Dr. Reigelmann. I've been told you were a shining star among your peers, the best Plastic Surgeon in your Fatherland. But, then, the world is full of hurting people. If not Germany, have you given any thought to where? England? France? The Netherlands? I hear its nice there."

"Maybe to a place where a man can start over clean," said Max. "I'm thinking of going to America."

September 1952, Bowery, New York City

New York City's skid row was blustery and cold as Leo Rosenbaum shifted his weight from foot to foot and surveyed the flapjacks of magazines and stacks of newspapers anchored with bricks at *McCormick's News Stand*. The garish comic book magazines strung on wire from the lip of its roof fluttered like lingerie in the breeze. The sky was overcast and threatened snow. The sound of the '50 Chevrolet Bel Air as it pulled up to the curb in front of the newsstand, was muffled and negligible. The reporter stood with his hands in his heaviest overcoat and wondered if McCormick would ever look up from placing more copies of the *New York Daily News* on its appointed pile next to the cash register.

"Could you hurry up, Michael," he hissed under his breath and stamped his feet. "It's freezing out here."

McCormick did not look up. To Leo's right side stood a heavily wrapped woman in her thirties wearing a fur cap, with an eight year old boy in an oversized coat who was most likely her son. Next to her, an old man with the yarmulke, long, black coat and hat, beard and side curls of an orthodox Hassidic Jew. Leo glanced down at the pile of *Times* newspapers—the headline declared that the secrets to building the atomic bomb were in jeopardy of being stolen by another country.

"Young man," the woman in the fur hat said as she waved a copy of *Redbook* at McCormick. "Young man, could I please buy this? We are in a hurry. We don't want to be late for my son's school."

Her son's rosy young face was buried in a copy of a comic book titled *Adventures into the Unknown,* that he knew his mother would not buy for him. Rosenbaum noticed, with some pleasure, that the Jewish man had opened a copy of the reporter's own *Tog Morgen Zhurnal.* McCormick either did not hear the woman or was too engrossed in adding copies of the *New York Daily News* to its place on the newsstand's counter, that he still did not look up.

The passenger's door to the Chevrolet swung open and a big, husky man appropriately dressed against the cold stepped out of the car, closed the door, and began to move around it to the sidewalk as a taxi cab also pulled over to the curb about thirty feet north of the Chevrolet.

The husky man who briskly rounded the front of the Bel Air with both of his hands shoved into the pockets of his coat and with his hat pulled down tight against the breeze was a single-minded and determined Carlos Valentine. He left a cloud of condensed breath behind him hanging in the air.

As Leo glanced his way, the reporter's blood turned to ice in his veins as both fury and fear turned to bitter bile in his stomach.

McCormick looked up.

"Oh, hey, good morning, Mr. Rosenbaum," he said cheerfully. "Great day if you're a penguin!"

Leo jerked his head in Carlos' direction and hissed, "Michael. Trouble."

McCormick followed the reporter's line of sight and whispered, "Damn."

Without hesitation, Carlos walked up to the boy and snatched the comic book out of his hands.

"Hey!" the kid shouted and reached out with both hands to reclaim the magazine.

"Hay is for horses," Carlos said, and shoved him, hard. Surprised, the boy stumbled back several feet and fell heavily with a thud, elbows first, to the sidewalk. Valentine slowly ripped the comic book in half for the drama of it and let the breeze carry the torn pages away.

"Get lost, brat" he said to the kid where the boy lay, tears welling up in his eyes.

"Jimmie, Jimmie," his mother cried out and threw her magazine down on the counter. Her arms open to embrace him, she ran awkwardly to him, knelt on the sidewalk and cradled his head in her arms. She looked up with fear and hatred at Valentine, stroking the boy's hair with one hand, her own eyes filmed with tears.

"Why did you do that?" she demanded. "Why? He wasn't doin' nothin' to you."

"Hey, I'm just helping out, lady," snarled Valentine. "He's rottin' his brain with that stuff. Now get lost, th' both of ya!!"

His head slightly lowered to his chest and his eyes afire, the DeSalvio torpedo slowly turned to Rosenbaum who had spread his legs apart to anchor his weight against what surely would follow.

"You. Nose-baum. Yer coming with me," Carlos snapped. "No ifs, buts, or nuts about it. Unless you want me to do to you what I did to your misses. Let's move it."

"You bastard," Leo hissed, his face cold and bloodless.

"Hey rat-face," said Valentine over his shoulder to the car without turning away from the reporter, "I'm famous! Th' guy knows me!"

From where he stood behind his cash register, McCormick let his left arm fall to his side.

"I've got a gun in my coat pocket leveled at your paper boy there, Jew boy," said Carlos. "If he gets any idea about grabbin' that baseball bat he keeps under the register, or you get any funny ideas... "

McCormick slowly raised his left arm.

The Hasidim Jew dropped his copy of the *Tog*, spun to his left side and pulled at .38 revolver out of his pocket.

"Don't move! Police!" he shouted.

Danny Costello stepped briskly from behind the enclosed end of the newsstand, behind the policeman with a blackjack in his right hand, and clubbed him in the back of his head.

"Oof!" The policeman fell like a sack of wet cement to the sidewalk.

The taxi pulled away from the curb and passed the newsstand, the Chevrolet, and the three DeSalvio thugs, picking up speed as it did so.

"As I was sayin'," resumed Carlos, "'Knife' Randuzzi is squattin' in the car with the nose of a machine gun stickin' out th' window as backup. So, shut up and move out, nose-baum."

Reluctantly, Leo walked to the car with Valentine following him. He opened the door and got into the back seat of the Bel Air, followed by the thug who slammed the door shut behind them. Costello, only moments behind them, plugged himself into the passenger's side of the Bel Air.

"Dammit," McCormick cursed as he vaulted, straight armed, over the counter of his newsstand and ran to the side of the fallen policeman as the black Chevrolet jerked away from the curb. As the owner of the newsstand did so, the mother was gently lifting her crying son from the sidewalk.

As it left the scene, the taxi, ahead of the Bel Air, swung around the corner and screeched to a stop at the curb. The cabbie threw open his door, and trotted to a police call box on the sidewalk with his right hand shoved deep in his pants pocket.

As the cabbie reached the box, he pulled a small key out of his pocket. He stuck it into the lock on the door to the call box, twisted the key, and opened the box, snatching the telephone from its cradle.

"Hello! Hello! Hello!" he barked into the mouthpiece.

"The Snake is struck," he hissed into the telephone.

It was Hank, the hack.

Chapter Twelve

January 1950, Manhattan, New York City

The red headed woman descended the stairs into the subway station, the sway of her hips and her shoulder-length hair accented by her descent. A train bellowed a warning and bellowed it again as it rumbled into view, slowed, and finally stopped with a metallic screech of its brakes.

The subway smelled like unwashed flesh and metal. There was tile everywhere like in a bathroom. The train's multiple doors squealed open to spit out a wave of diverse men, women, and some children like multicolored dollops of paint slapped onto a canvas. They did not so much disembark as they were splashed out through the doors onto the landing platform.

With each of her rhythmic steps, the red head on the stairs thought *this will never end, this will never end, they know my face, they know my name, they will never stop, this will never end,* as she cast furtive and secret glances around her like an invisible net.

As the train disgorged its passengers, the red headed woman stopped at the ticket booth with several other potential passengers behind her and slid several coins through its little window.

"Two tokens, please," she said, demure and cool in appearance, the very picture of poise and sophistication. Inside, her heart was beating like a trip hammer.

If she was right, he was here. And she was the one he hunted.

The fingers that pushed the tokens back through the window were short and fat and the fingernails were uneven and seemed somehow unclean. It was not the first pudgy fingers or the first tickets she had bought in her long and desperate flight across Italy, France, the Netherlands, England and finally to America and Gotham. She cast furtive glances around her like a net, but he was felt, not seen.

Disgorged, the train bellowed a warning and bellowed it again as it lurched forward and began to pick up speed as it left its position next to the loading platform.

The young, red-headed woman moved to the row of turnstiles and dropped her token into the narrow slot of the one closest to her, then pushed through the restraining bar. She heard the low rumble building in volume like a distant earthquake as another subway train bellowed a warning and bellowed it again as it approached the loading platform. The low rumble had become a click clack..click...clack click....clack that accented the low murmur of the milling sea of waiting men, women and children as the train rumbled out of the black maw of its tunnel, approaching the landing. The crowd, of which she was now a part, irresistibly carried her along in its ebb and flow as she looked up and behind her.

He was there, at the mouth of the stairs into the subway, descending.

She glanced at the on-rushing steel behemoth as she was pushed and pulled against the waiting crush of human bodies thinking *hurry. Hurry up, hurry, hurry up.*

She watched as the train's illuminated windows began to slowly pass her, slowing, the people inside as motionless as mannequins, and she began to follow the train, walking quickly,click clack..click...clack click.... clack pushing her way through the crowd.

He was there, now, tall and bald, at the bottom of the stairs. She could not see him, but she knew.

A door in the train opened and the crowd did not so much board it as the soon-to-be passengers exploded like a geyser through the opening, but she was too far back, and the red-headed woman knew she wouldn't make it in. Her eyes darted here, there, everywhere, looking for escape into the train, but she knew, instinctively, that she was too late. The train bellowed a warning and bellowed it again.

He was coming. Much closer now.

The red-headed woman was trotting now almost like a quarterback on a broken field as the crowd boarded and thinned out on the loading platform somewhat, the sway of her shoulder-length hair and the suitcase in

"Two tokens, please."

her hand accented by her movement as she dodged, feinted, stumbled, re-gained her footing as she ran, pushing surprised and angry passengers out of her way, as she ran right up to the subway train as its final door closed. She was trapped.

She saw him, in a flash, pushing his way through the crowd, following her.

The train bellowed a final warning and bellowed it again as it slowly pulled away from the landing and she ran again, increasing her speed with the speed of the train, looking frantically around her as she did so for something, for anything that would save her. Behind her, he had broken free from the crowd as well and was also running, running, running.

She knew her chance for escape was one in a million so the long, metal rod stacked against the subway wall in a cluster of tools seemed like a miracle as, without reducing her speed, she snatched it up and looked be-hind her.

The bald headed man was near, now, very near, running. The train click clack....click...clack click..clack was picking up speed and closing the dis-tance between her and it as she was thinking *this is it this is it this is it* but calmly now, judging the distance, judging the timing, judging the insanity of her choice as the bald man yelled.

"Stop!" he screamed at the top of his lungs. "Stop!"

The red-headed woman at that second swung towards the train and the tracks and picked up her speed and the metal behemoth seemed to breathe fire down her neck click clack....click...clack click..clack and the bald man was only yards behind her as she jammed the rod against the ce-ment walkway and pole vaulted across the tracks to the other side.

She dropped the rod and ran.

At that same second, the train blocked her from view and the bald headed man stumbled, fell and slid forward in her wake, only stopping himself with his outstretched arms and his hands on the rail of the on-coming metal monster.

He looked up into the gigantic face of certain death.

The train thundered.

 click clack....click...clack click..clack

He jerked his hands away.

 click clack....click...clack click..clack

The train thundered past.

The bald man lay for long moments on the walk way, breathing heavily, before he could stand up. As he stood up, the final cars of the train passed him.

The other side of the landing was empty.

She was gone.

The yellow taxi stopped at the curb, and the red-headed woman opened her door and stepped out onto a Manhattan sidewalk at the foot of a sky-scraper. She closed her door and stepped to the cabbie's window. Bending at the waist as he rolled down his window, she handed him several bills.

"Thanks," Greta Hoffmeyer said, and smiled. "It's just where they said it would be." In her head, she added *the they being my detectives thank god.*

She walked to the entrance to the skyscraper and looked at a plaque screwed into the wall faced with marble next to the door.

The small, bronze plaque read: *Dr. Max Riegelmann. Plastic Surgeon.*

September 1952, Bowery, New York City

Friedrich Nietzsche wrote *"That which does not kill us makes us stronger." That is a lie.*

A lie is like a Kabuki mask that we wear to protect ourselves. Nietzsche wore that Kabuki mask to hide the truth. He was sick and weak.

We all wear masks like Nietzsche.

The faded green "Star" taxi that was an embarrassment to taxis everywhere pulled over and stopped at the curb in front of Doctor Joseph Eacobacci who, waiting for the fifth time on the sidewalk, stepped back instinctively even though he was well familiar with the routine now.

The psychologist who took a secret pleasure in looking more like a stevedore, or lumberjack, or a motorcycle thug than like his hero, Carl Jung, wore the same short-sleeved black shirt with vertical strips and beige khakis that he'd worn at his first unofficial kidnapping. After all, he didn't want to look like a psychologist, all things considered. Beneath the front of his shirt and tucked into the waist of his jeans, he still carried his pearl handled revolver, and wore a pair of sunglasses on the top of his head that were quickly becoming unseasonal.

The back passenger's door of the taxi had been flung open, but not by the old blind man called Admiral Bridges. Eacobacci leaned forward at the waist to get a better view of the back seat, and saw only a black blindfold laying there. As he did so, the opaque glass partition finished its rise to the cab's ceiling and sealed itself. Eacobacci sighed, swung onto the bench seat, and picked up the blindfold.

"Is this still necessary?" he objected to the driver on the opposite side of the glass separating the cabbie's from the passenger's bench seat. He recognized the song on the radio, "Jambalaya" by Joe Stafford, even though it was muffled by the glass hiding its driver. If he'd learned one thing from his multiple sessions with Snake it was that the cabbie loved popular music.

"Put it on," said the un-seeable hack, without the useless effort of turning to face the psychologist. "You become a Prima Dona since last time, maybe?"

Eacobacci began to tie the blindfold around his eyes.

"What's to keep me from leaving a little crack in the blindfold so I can see out," he said to the cabbie just to make conversation.

"The glass is a two way mirror, doc. I can see everything you do."

"Okay. Then what's to stop me from just opening my door and tumbling out before we gain too much speed?"

"I've got an automatic door locking doohickey up here, that's what, Mr. Know-It-All," said the cabbie.

As the hack said it, the psychologist watched as the knob that locks and unlocks a door popped up on its own, and then down again, locking his door and the door opposite him, then up and then down. "I shoulda guessed," he exclaimed. "Just considering my options. Will we be having more of the silly cloak and dagger nonsense today?"

"No nonsense to it," replied the hack. "There are certain unsavory elements that would love nothing better than to find my lady and do her or any of her friends—that includes me—or acquaintances—that's you—bodily harm. So this set up is for your safety and mine, doc. Why not sit back and enjoy the music?"

"Sure, why not. Since that now, what were my voluntary sessions with the mysterious lady called Snake, have become mandatory, any chance that I can at least know the name of the man I'm talking with?"

"Nope."

"Snake's name?"

"Not even if I knew it. I like to call her lady, and she likes it to. Why don't you try that? L. A. D. Y. Lady."

"Okay. Okay. I get your drift. Do you mind if I ask you a question?"

"Nope."

"You seem like a normal enough guy. How did you get involved with this mystery woman who dresses like a dominatrix and steals from thieves and kills cops?"

"She didn't kill anything, doc. She's got a strict rule against doing that. The cop thing was an accident."

"And just how do you know that?"

"She told me, and she doesn't lie to her associates. And I heard it first hand from an eyewitness."

"I'll accept that for now..." began Eacobacci, only to have this thought cut short.

"Yeah. Like you got a choice."

"I'll accept your word, but that doesn't answer my question."

"Well..." began the hack, and then stopped for some unexplained reason. "I did a stint in Korea; got a steel plate in my head as a souvenir. And the only job I could find when I got out was hacking. Just about enough income to keep me scraping the bottom of the barrel. So, at first, I did it for the money, just like everybody does everything for the money, doc."

"How did you find her?"

"Didn't. She found me. I took a fare, and looked back, and there she was, dressed like she was going to a funeral or something, all in black with a black veil over her face. We got to talking, and she asked me if I'd be interested in being a sorta chauffeur for a salary that would make a horse choke."

"So all this secrecy and skating on the edge of the law is just for the bucks."

"At first. I got to kind of liking her, and, frankly, when it got a little more involved, I found out that I had been missing the excitement of Korea. So it's sorta of a win, win for me, doc. Now, I get to ask you one, right?"

"Right."

"Why are you doing this? I mean, I know about how you feel grateful for her saving your daughter and all of that. But you are getting in pretty deep yourself, you know. Or do you?"

There was a long pause before Eacobacci answered.

"I know."

"We're both men here, doc, and no one else is listening. I'm guessing there's the daughter thing alright, and I get that, but you'd also like to get to know what's underneath all of that leather, if you know what I mean, and you do, eh?"

"Then we've both made some bad assumptions, today, my mystery friend. My relationship with your boss is strictly clinical."

"Yeah, right. One of the things I learned in our country's 'police action', doc, is that we all wear masks to hide who we really are. But masks are lies.

You know that. But we all wear masks, so I get it."

"I love my wife," said the doctor. "That's not a Kabuki mask."

But it bothered him somewhat that he could lie so easily.

Fat Al squatted at the entrance to his grocery store on the Bowery to pick up his morning newspaper because he could not bend at the waist without falling over. He wore a shirt untucked that was so large that it almost looked like a smock for the same reason that he squatted. Fat Al was very fat.

It was 4:10am and, as was his routine, he reentered his shop and locked it behind him because Fat Al didn't open the grocery until 5:00am and he liked to begin his day with a cup of strong, black coffee, ten or so Danish pastries or donuts, and his newspaper. It was a twenty-two year old routine that would almost never vary for his entire life until he would die of a heart attack sometime in the future—but not this morning.

It had to be a better day than yesterday because, yesterday, late in the evening, he had been robbed at gun point and then robbed again when that horror of a madwoman, Snake, had robbed the robbers. They had gotten away with more than $2,000 because Fat Al hadn't made his deposit at the bank yet for the day.

So he sat down on a stool by his cash register where his cup of coffee and Danish waited for him, and rolled off the rubber band that held the newspaper together, still trying to console himself over his immense loss. He took a sip of coffee. It felt good going down his gullet. Then he took off a second rubber band before his second sip, and only noticed as he removed the third rubber band that something wasn't right. Three rubber bands? Routine will do that to a man, especially a man as old as Fat Al.

He opened the newspaper only to discover an envelope inside. Thinking that it was his notice to renew his subscription, he tore off the end of the envelope and shook it vigorously to remove its contents.

More than $2,000 in crisp, new bills fell out of the envelope onto the newspaper.

Fat Al was more than surprised. It was the exact amount of money that had been stolen from his shop yesterday. It made no sense. He quickly stuck the bills into the front, right pocket of his jeans, and, illogically, quickly looked around to make sure that no one in the locked shop had seen him doing it. Mixed in with the surprise was joy.

He got up from his seat and moved to the front door of his shop. He unlocked the door and opened his shop for business.

Fat Al wondered about the mysterious $2,000 all day long, trying to figure out what had actually happened.

Late that evening, he realized that if he didn't report the cash to the insurance company, the payoff from the robbery would almost double what he put in his pants pocket earlier.

His only regret was that he couldn't tell anyone about what would remain the most amazing event in his otherwise mundane life.

Chapter Thirteen

February 1950, Manhattan, New York City

Doctor Max Riegelmann leaned back in his chair in his small office, laced his fingers together, and closed his eyes. It was his routine to rest for ten minutes between each consultation and thirty minutes between out-patient procedures to meditate and count his blessings, and. although he knew he only had one or possibly two consultations left for the day, he had no intention of breaking his relatively new, life-affirming habit. The office was cool and quiet; there was no window onto the sometimes invigorating and sometimes depressing turmoil of life outside on the streets of Manhattan.

In the years since he had fled Germany, Max had repressed the memory of the horrors of the war so deep inside his subconscious mind that those memories now lived only in rare nightmares and cold sweats. He had taught himself to focus on the now and on the future; it had taken some time. The only image that still flickered uninvited and randomly in his otherwise highly structured days was that of a woman whose long, blonde hair cascaded to perfect, gently rounded shoulders, whose large, deep-blue eyes had once penetrated into the depths of his soul, whose high, rosy cheek bones, flawless almond skin, full strawberry lips, and heart-shaped jaw had burned themselves into his soul forever.

A knock on his door broke his thoughts.

"Excuse me, Doctor Riegelmann," inquired the familiar and muffled female voice on the other side of the door, "your last consultation is here in room seven."

Go away, Mildred, he said inside his head. "I'll be right there," he said aloud.

When he opened the door, he looked up at the nurse in her thirties, who was waiting for him in her traditional plain, white dress, carrying a clipboard and forcing a weary smile on her tired face.

"I hope I didn't startle you," she said. She looked down at her clipboard, turned over a sheet of paper, and read aloud, "This patient is named Marilyn Paige, doctor. Twenty-eight years old, in excellent health and, if I may say so, probably the last woman alive who needs a face lift."

"You know that it isn't that unusual," was his measured response. "Sometimes, the need may not be physical, but emotional, and still just as real to them."

As they walked down the short hallway together to room seven, Max berated himself for thinking of Mildred as plain. Unlike almost every other woman, she did not startle when she looked down at him, or suppress repulsion at his physical appearance, but treated him with a casual indifference that at least manifested itself in courtesy, kindness, and politeness.

He would have been a fool to expect more from any woman. After all, the love of his life had died with the last bombing of Berlin, and there would never be another.

"Thank you, nurse Mildred; I'll call if I need you," he said as they stopped before the door to the waiting room. He smiled. She turned and walked away. He opened the door to room seven.

His patient sat in a simple blue dress on the examination table with her back to the doctor. She wore a modestly expensive bracelet of precious stones inlaid in a low grade of gold that Riegelmann did not notice.

"Good afternoon," said Max. "I'm doctor Max Riegelmann. How are you today?"

The woman who had attractive, long, red hair slowly turned around.

"Hello, Max," she answered in German.

Max's reaction to her was no different than if an orthodox Jew had watched Jesus Christ step out of the tomb.

It was Gretchen Lagle.

Max, eagerly and in still some minor state of shock and denial, rolled a small metal stool to the side of the examination table and sat down as Gretchen, cool, demure, ineffable, and controlled, lied in their native language about the painful and bleak years of life without him.

"They'd been watching me as well as you, sweetheart," she continued with a muted pain in her voice, "and I later found out that we'd both been arrested as traitors and conspirators by the Nazis at almost the same time.

That's the last time I heard your name spoken except in my heart, dearest, until I came to America.

"Although I had no idea what they were talking about, sweetheart, I was charged with participating in an attempt to assassinate Hitler, and I was tortured."

"Gretchen," whispered Max as tears welled up in his eyes. "I-I am so sorry."

"I know you never intended to hurt me. They took me to some secret place. But, no matter what they did to me, I had nothing to tell them, and sometimes fainted from the pain. It was my only release. But the time between each session grew longer, and longer, and I could sense a growing confusion in my tormentors that must have been from the horrendous bombings of Berlin that seemed to increase ten-fold every day. They must have known the Allies were near."

"I was taken to Sachsenhausen," said Max."

"Sachsenhausen? I don't think I've ever heard of that."

"A concentration camp."

"A what, Max? What is a concentration camp?"

"It doesn't matter now, Gretchen. I'm sorry I interrupted. Please. Continue."

"I don't like to dwell on the horrors of that time—I'm sure you understand that, sweetheart?—so eventually, from some sort of oversight on their part, I was left alone one time, and was able to escape. And by begging and sometimes even stealing something to eat and drink, and walking or hitching a ride on a farmer's truck or a horse-drawn wagon, I finally found my way to a relative in France. With his help and the help of his family, I was eventually able to find a job and build a new life. But after so many years in France, I could never stop thinking about my Max.

"I thought you were dead."

"I was, Gretchen, without you. I thought you were dead too."

"I thought you were dead until just a day ago when, by the hand of God, I saw an article in a newspaper about you. It was one of the greatest surprises of my entire life."

Max stood up. "I have put the past behind me, Gretchen. Now, we're together again, and that's what matters the most, and we can live a safe and happy life here."

Gretchen lowered her head to her chest for a moment. Max bit his lower lip and turned his face away from her as she did so. When she looked at the surgeon again, there was fear in her eyes.

"Max, I'm not so sure. An underground group has formed, still loyal to the Third Reich and Hitler's memory, Nazi sympathizers that call themselves Neo-Nazis. Max, I don't know this for sure, but I think they are hunting for 'traitors' like me, and maybe even for you. They want me dead."

"You have seen them, Gretchen?"

"Well, no. Not really. I have read about them, and heard about them in news reels. I sometimes feel them, Max, with a woman's intuition and I am afraid for my life."

"Not in American. Not with me, now, Gretchen. Where are you staying?"

"At a hotel in the Bowery, sweetheart. A flophouse called the Sunshine Hotel." She lowered her face again and blushed. "It's all I can afford right now."

Max opened his arms.

"No, you aren't. You're coming home with me."

A light snow began to fall as the crowd from the Alvin theater on West 52nd Street began to spill out of the doors of the theater to stop cold and surprised under the artificial stars embedded in the underside of its broad entrance. Their exuberant applause still rang in their ears. The audience that had just enjoyed the play *A Tree Grows in Brooklyn,* still flush with pleasure from their experience, was now somewhat perturbed by the big, individual snow flakes that were already gathering at the bottom edges of the recessed posters on either side of the entrance. Women in their finest gowns, great coats, and hats pulled up their collars around their necks and tied scarves, if they had them, over their hairdos, and fussed about the inconvenience as, one by one, men peeled off of the edges of the crowd to race into the street in search of their automobiles or to tap on the window of one of the many cabs waiting at the curb in front of the *Alvin.*

In the trapped current of the crowd, a spirited and happy Gretchen Lagle snuggled close against Max's overcoat with one of her arms tightly interlaced in his and she looked down into his smiling face.

"Oh, wasn't Shirley Booth just wonderful, Max," she said. "I've never had more fun. It almost makes me want to go back on the stage."

The surgeon met her statement with a puzzled expression.

"*Back* on the stage, Gretchen? When were you ever on the stage?"

"Oh, in school, silly. When I was a teenager, I played the lead in *Cinderella.*"

"I wish I had known you then and seen you in your play, sweetheart," he said and began to gently pull away from her arm. "Listen, if I hurry, I may be able to get one of those cabs and get you out of this dreadful weather."

Her grip tightened and her face changed also instantly from joy to deep concern.

"No, Max, don't," she protested. "I'm frightened. Don't leave just yet."

"Why on earth not?"

"It's...that...feeling...again. I think someone is...watching us."

Max looked up into her beautiful, sincere face with am irritation that had only grown in their three days together.

"Darling. Please. Not that, again. There's no one looking at you."

Using the movement of her eyes to indicate a location, she said, "Over there. Don't turn around. He'll see you."

He followed her eyes to a man leaning against a wall of the theater with a newspaper opened that obscured his face. Over the top edge of the paper, Max saw that he wore a modest dark hat and suit, and the handle of an umbrella was hooked over his left forearm.

"Him?" he asked, nodding his head to indicate the gentleman. "Darling, he's just reading a newspaper and waiting for a taxi."

"No he isn't. He's looking for me. I just know it. Can't you believe me?"

"Gretchen, I don't say this to hurt you, but you are becoming a little paranoid about this. He's probably waiting out the snow and waiting for the crowd to thin out before leaving."

The tears welled up in Gretchen's eyes and she snuggled even tighter against Max. She gingerly touched the corner of her left eye, then her nose, and then her check with the gloved finger pads of her free hand.

"Just a little here, and here, and here, Max. The only way I can be sure; the one way I can escape is for you to change my face—just a little, sweetheart. I'll still be your Gretchen. You can make certain of that. Just change my face enough so I won't be recognized...by them...anymore. Please, Max. "

A woman pressed against her because of the crowd gave Gretchen a puzzled and disapproving look. Gretchen pulled Max away from the woman, forcing her way closer to the mouth of the entrance.

"I would rather cut off my own arm, Gretchen, than to change one thing about the face I love. We've talked about this so many times in the last few days that it's really becoming....annoying. I don't want to talk about it now."

"But, sweetheart, it would be such a small thing for you. Just think of it. I could look more like the fantasy lover you—every man— has. And it would free me from what you think is my paranoia."

"You *are* the fantasy lover I always dreamed about. Would you like a little snack or a drink before we go home. We can stop off..."

"Max, please don't change the subject. This is really, really important to me. You said you love me..."

"With all of my heart. They have a great, light souffle at the..."

"If you truly love me, Maxey, you'll do this for me."

"Look...look!" the surgeon exclaimed with a faux excitement and pulled his arm free of Gretchen, "There's an empty taxi!"

He waved a hand above his head as he struggled through the slowly thinning crowd towards the curb. "Here, over here!" he shouted illogically because he knew he couldn't be heard over the low murmur of the crowd and through the metal door of a taxi cab. But he shouted nonetheless.

"Taxi! Taxi!"

Just as the surgeon broke free of the crowd, the last taxi stationed in front of the theater pulled slowly away from the curb. Max dropped his arm. Several large fat snowflakes struck and temporarily clung to his cheek. He turned around and back to the crowd, searching for his lover.

"Gretchen..." he began, but stopped.

She had not followed him.

Max sighed deeply as more men spun off the edges of the crowd onto the sidewalk and women frowned and clutched the ends of the scarves over the heads, or patted at their uncovered hair in anticipated disaster. Max sighed again and began to worm his way back into the milling crowd.

The man leaning against the wall of the theater folded up his newspaper, stuck it under his left arm, and ran his right hand over his bald head.

Then Ben Alashee walked away.

Chapter Fourteen

March 1950, Manhattan, New York City

Max didn't know it was the last mistake he would make in his life.

The only sounds in the otherwise tiny, silent room that night were a thin stream of water gushing from a faucet into a porcelain sink as Jo Stafford sang "You Belong To Me" and Doctor Max Rieglemann vigorously scrubbed his hands. The dial on the Bakelite radio perched on the metal shelf attached to the wall over the sink was set on WKBD. Max had intentionally developed the habit of listening to the mindless, popular songs of Johnnie Ray, Rosemary Clooney, Eddie Fisher, Patti Page and many others not only in the little room where he prepared himself for surgery but on a second radio in his office, and even on a radio at home. He listened to help drain away the tension that was just the natural consequence of his work.

These were the only sounds in his office because the surgeon had made certain that every member of his staff had gone home long ago. He also knew that the only people left in the entire skyscraper were a handful of bored, indifferent janitors and clueless guards on different floors. So there was no reason for his hands to tremble slightly; nevertheless, they did.

He hummed the tune that Stafford sang as he scrubbed his hands. His surgical mask hung loose around his neck.

Gretchen Lagle could hear nothing where she lay anesthetized on the single operating table next to a small, metal table on wheels that held a polished tray full of a sterilized assortment of scalpels. It occurred to Max as he prepared himself that it was the only time in days that he hadn't had to endure her constant, nagging, begging, manipulative plea for a new face. He smiled, but just for a fleeting moment and not because he was happy as he examined his fingernails to make sure they were pristine.

Except for the slow rise and fall of her chest as she breathed, Gretchen did not move under the sanitized white sheet that covered everything but her head. She had cut her red hair short herself, so Max wouldn't know it was a wig. Beneath the sheet and without Max's knowledge, she wore a modestly expensive bracelet of precious stones inlaid in a low grade of gold on her right wrist. Her hair was pulled back from her forehead and securely covered by a cap.

Max was holding his hands up to dry them on a towel hanging from a ring next to the sink when a reporter on the radio followed the song with breaking news.

"In an effort to alert the public and aid in capturing an international war criminal, it has been announced today that a deadly, former Gestapo spy is at large in Gotham. This woman is in her early thirties, and has gone under the names of Greta Hoffmeyer, Lise Meitner, Bertha Giehse, and Gertrude Lagle in the past to hide her true identity. She is described as of medium height with a very attractive body, but further description is almost useless because she is a master of disguise. This is a treacherous woman directly and indirectly responsible for the deaths of many World War II patriots of many nations. You are encouraged to watch for the following list of possible clues to...."

"Tell me something I don't already know," said Max under his breath.

The reporter's words carried no weight for the surgeon as Max ground his teeth and his twin brother's severed head rolled across the floor leaving a trail of blood and a Nazi fist knocked out his teeth and crushed his cheek bone and slashed him with a knife and lashed the fleshy hump on his back and dried his hands in the folds of the towel and the needle-sharp teeth of starving dogs tore him into bleeding ribbons and he ground his teeth and the bared fangs of a snake were thrust into his face and he ground his teeth and he screamed and screamed and screamed and screamed and dried his hands with the towel in the ring next to the sink.

His eyes fixed and dead, and his face covered with hot beads of sweat from the overwhelming horror of his last days in Germany, Max inspected his hands and then his forearms to make sure that they were thoroughly clean and dried, and stopped twisting his arms only when he came to the branded numbers that for so many years he had tried and failed to scrub away—665.

He looked at the raised numbers.

And Max thought *I'm still one short of the number of man.*

Then he pulled out a pair of latex gloves from a box attached to the opposite wall next to the sink, and methodically rolled them onto his hands. He picked up the loose laces of his surgical mask and tied them around the back of his head.

Holding his forearms and hands vertically against his chest, he pushed through the swinging doors that separated the sink from the operating room with his elbows.

They swung in diminishing arcs after his passing.

Behind the surgeon, Johnnie Ray was crooning "The Little White Cloud That Cried" on WKBD.

In the long days that followed the operation, Max had spent much of the time meticulously planning it down to the finest detail. He was even wearing a suit under his white smock that looked exactly like the one that he had worn when he had first interviewed her in Germany.

Max turned his record player on where it sat on a small mahogany table against a wall and placed its phonographic needle on the disc resting on its turntable. The melancholy chords of Gretchen's favorite song, Beethoven's *Für Elise,* swelled up and filled his modest but carefully arranged living room.

Gretchen sat in a comfortable, armless chair in the middle of the room with her hands resting on her lap. She held a small hand mirror by its handle. Max had placed a small, metallic table on rollers next to her chair. On it lay a pair of scissors. She wore a simple, white shift and black pumps, and her red hair spiked out of the holes cut out of the bandages that completely covered her head except for slits for her eyes, nostrils, and mouth. She smelled like almonds.

"Good morning, Gretchen," said the surgeon as he approached her. "I hope you're feeling well today, sweetheart."

"It...hurts, Max," she answered, her voice somewhat muffled and constrained by the bandages. "But...I'm...excited."

Max picked up the scissors. *Für Elise* swelled and filled his living room.

"Although it has been two weeks, darling, it will take some additional time to heal. You will still feel some diminishing discomfort for several weeks. This is completely normal for extensive plastic surgery. If the pain is unendurable, I do have some pills, but I use them sparingly because they can be addictive, and there are some ointments that can quicken the healing process, if they are necessary."

He snipped the edge of a bandage at the edge of her chin just in front of her ear, then snipped and snipped again until the swath came free. He unrolled the bandage, following it around her head, and rolling if up like a scroll as he did so. Then he unceremoniously dropped the roll on the floor.

"I have done my best. I have tried to bring out the real you, darling."

"Thank you..." whispered Gretchen. I love you, too, darling." *Für Elise* swelled.

"Sssssh. Don't try to talk now, sweetheart. It moves the wrappings."

Max snipped through another length of cotton swath and began to remove it.

"It is not unusual for a patient to be somewhat surprised and even disappointed initially, Gretchen, at their new appearance. We all have a picture in our heads of how we ideally would like to look."

Max dropped a bandage scroll on the floor at his feet.

"We are almost done. There, and there. Your mirror is in your hands, dear."

Max stepped back and pulled a revolver from beneath his white smock.

"Take a moment to open your eyes. The light may initially blind you."

He took three clumsy steps back from where she sat on the chair in a little nest of white scrolls on the floor.

"An eye for an eye..." Max said, his voice shaking, and put the pudgy finger of his right hand through the trigger guard. "I always knew, sweetheart, even before you knocked on my door and came back from the dead. I tried to forget, but I couldn't.

"I didn't want it to happen this way."

"It…hurts, Max."

Tears streamed down his scarred and broken face that had been beaten black and blue and lacerated by the Nazis. His hand holding the revolver visibly shook.

"A tooth for a tooth," he said as his voice fell dead and Max leveled the gun at Gretchen's face. "When the Nazis were torturing me in Berlin, they told me it was you.

"That you betrayed me.

"That you turned in Franz."

Ignoring his words and wearing an excited, great smile, Gretchen began to open her eyes and raise the mirror to her face.

"No," he exclaimed as the reality of his work with scalpel and stitch and acid pushed it way up through his hatred and denial. "No. What have I done?"

Gretchen held the mirror in front of her face.

Max turned the revolver, placing the cold barrel of the gun on his right temple.

"Gretchen," he said and pulled the trigger and blew his brains out.

Only one heard the staccato report of the revolver that sounded like a rim shot on a snare drum.

Only one heard Max's corpse hit the floor with a thud.

September 1952, Bowery, New York City

The double rap on Lieutenant Manning's door was not unexpected, so he did not look up from the pile of papers in front of him. He stopped writing with the ink pen in his right hand. He sat behind an old, scarred, oak desk that had been at the Bowery's ninth precinct long before Manning had been born.

"Come in," he barked. "Make it short."

The policeman who had failed to stop Rosenbaum's abduction from McCormick's newsstand opened the door and reluctantly stepped inside the room. He held his cap on his chest with both hands and his head was lowered.

"Douglas reporting as requested, sir," he said. "I can come back if you're busy."

Manning did not look up as he returned to writing.

"Sit down, Douglas," he said and nodded in the direction of a chair placed in front of his desk. "We need to talk."

Douglas sat down and placed his cap on the edge of his superior officer's desk. Lieutenant Manning looked up.

"Get your cap off of my desk, Douglas."

Douglas snatched his cap from the desk and, failing to find another place for it, set it in his lap.

"How long have you been with us, Douglas?"

"Five years next month, sir."

"Do you like it here, Douglas?"

"Y-yes..." the policeman stammered, and swallowed hard."...sir."

"Good, good," the lieutenant said as, leaning forward and placing his elbows on his desk, he intertwined his fingers. "Glad to hear it. I like my men to like what they do. Now, using as few words as you possibly can, I'd like to hear from your mouth just exactly what happened on your stake-out."

"I dressed up like a Hassidic Jew, sir..."

"Too many words. Try again."

"I pretended to be buying a magazine at Rosenbaum's favorite...

"You get one more chance, Douglas."

There was a long pause as the policeman struggled to understand what his commander wanted from him. Then an expression of calm replaced his fear as he said:

"I screwed up."

"That's it. That's what I wanted to hear. Yes, you did, Douglas. And when you screw up, try to guess who else also gets screwed."

His pause was painful before the policeman replied.

"You, sir?"

"Yes. Royally. And who else?"

"The precinct?"

"Yes, yes. I think you've got it now. And who else, Douglas?"

His last admission was like pulling teeth.

"E-every cop in Gotham?"

"And when are you going to screw up again, son?"

"Never, sir."

"That's exactly right. Because if you do, this little report I'm filling out will get submitted, and you will never do anything but catch stray cats and dogs with a net for the rest of your career. Do you understand that, Douglas?"

"Yes, sir."

Manning returned to writing on the uppermost piece of paper on the stack of papers before him.

"Get out," he said quietly. "And don't come back until Rosenbaum is toasting his toes in front of a fire at home, and you've delivered Snake's head to me on a platter."

The door to Manning's office opened and closed before the lieutenant had spoken the last word.

"Damn fools," he muttered to himself.

"He don't know me very well, do he."

Startled, Manning looked up to follow the sound of the disembodied, eerie voice like the weird hiss of a snake to the open window to the right side of his desk in the wall facing Bowery Street.

"Here's lookin' at me, kid." Snake said as she perched on the window frame in full regalia with her quarterstaff strapped to her back.

"Look!" she said, pointing at the ceiling, "it's a bird, it's a plane...it's... me!" She saluted the lieutenant smartly, then leapt gracefully and almost soundlessly to the floor.

At the same instant, Manning stood up straight from his desk, knocking his chair over backwards, and snatched his revolver from its holster.

At that same instant, Snake snapped the whip by its butt off of her hip, threw the thong back over her shoulder, then snapped it forward. Its popper snaked out and bit Manning's gun hand.

He barked, "Damn it" and dropped the revolver, clutching his stung hand as if it were on fire.

"Allow me to introduce myself," Snake said, and bowed at the waist. "My name is Puddintain. Ask me again, and I'll tell you the same. Do you want I should kiss it and make it all well?"

"How the Hell did you get up here," snarled Manning, rubbing his stung hand. "We're on the damn third floor!"

"Does Macy's tell Gimbel's?" asked Snake as she rolled the whip back into a circle without ever taking her eyes off of the lieutenant, and snapped it back on her hip.

Manning looked down at his revolver on the floor and then at the closed door to his office.

Snake extended her right arm and aimed the dart gun strapped there at Manning.

"No, no, no," said the leather-clad she-devil, waving a warning with her index finger. "I can have a dart in your neck that will temporarily paralyze you before you can even touch your toes, Lieutenant Manning. Yell for help? Reach for that gun? I wouldn't try either if I were you. But I don't plan on being you until next week."

"You're the maniac that killed one of my men," Manning snarled. "What the Hell are you doing here?"

"I kill no one," said Snake as she began to pace back in forth in front of Manning's desk. "Your rookie's death was an accident brought on by his own inexperience, and you know it, Tin Man, deep down where you used to have a heart.

"Sit down. It would be so nice if something made sense for a change, eh? Well, have I got a change for you. I am here because I know the location of something you want, you naughty boy. Me. And I know where something else you want is camped out, too. John, 'The Hammer,' Desalvio. I know where they both are, and I'll toss in Leo Rosenbaum with toasty toes just for fun. But you'll only get them all, honey, on my terms. Hi ho Silver, away!"

"This isn't a circus," said Manning, "and I don't negotiate with criminals in clown costumes. So get out."

"I know, sweetheart', that's why you'll negotiate with me. I'm not a clown. I'm the real deal. Now, why don't you'll shut up and sit down like I told you. Remember, there are many ways of going forward, but only one way of standing still."

"What the Hell does that mean?"

"Don't judge a book by its cover, sweetie pie. I only ask you to judge me by the enemies I have made."

Reluctantly, his eyes never leaving the woman in the Kabuki mask, Manning began to sit down in his chair.

"You're absolutely nuts," he said.

"We're all mad here," Snake said as she walked with the grace of a jungle cat to the chair facing Manning, sat down, and kicked up her legs, placing the heels of her boots on the edge of his desk.

"Of all the gin joints in all the towns in all the world, she walks into yours, eh, Lieutenant Manning?

"Now, this is what will happen."

Chapter Fifteen

With his back and also his left leg, bent at the knee and up against the slaughterhouse wall next to its entrance, Rat-faced "Knife" Randuzzi tapped raw tobacco from a tiny bag into the paper gutter in the cigarette paper he had formed with his thumb and the first two fingers of his left hand. It was early evening and cold as death, and he would have given almost anything to be warm and mostly drunk at *Sammy's Bowery Follies* with a pint of beer in his hand. His heavy overcoat did little to keep the brittle night air at bay, and just as he pulled the drawstring of his bag of tobacco closed with his teeth, it began to snow lightly.

"Wouldn't ya know it," he muttered to the night, "I can't buy a break."

The snow seemed half asleep as it drifted down, the dusting thickening even as he watched, threatening to become a white storm. It was then Knife saw a wizened old black man in a Fedora dressed in a second-hand, wrinkled suit, that had once been black, approaching him like a ghost out of the snow. The black man was tapping a cane in front of him carved from an oak branch that looked more like a cudgel. As he drew near, Randuzzi saw the bum was wearing sun glasses, his close-cropped hair was peppered with gray, and his mustache was unevenly trimmed.

"I know you," he said, dropping his left leg from the wall as he spoke and rolling his cigarette paper into a scroll. "You're that blind drunk that begs for change down on the Bowery. Where's your cane, and what th' Hell you doin' here?"

"If I'm not on the Bowery, I guess I'm lost," said The Admiral, and smiled as he continued to approach the hood. "Just like my old cane. When I lose something, it's kinda hard to find again. Oh well, it's not the first time."

"There ain't nothin' here," said Randuzzi, "but warehouses and this old abandoned slaughterhouse that's eatin' up my drinkin' time. There ain't no one here to beg for money, especially me. So it ain't your first; be sure you make it your last. I'm busy here."

"All I ask for is a dime for a hot cup of coffee and a sinker," said the Admiral, now very near the thug but not slowing his approach. "Just a plain doughnut for a starving old man, sir."

"Hey! Slow do..." Randuzzi began, but too late. The black man slammed into him even as Randuzzi cushioned the blow with his raised hands on the old man's chest. Knife shoved the old man back, hard!

"Hey, you damn idiot! Watch where you're goin'!!"

"But that's the point. I *can't* watch where I'm goin'," The Admiral grinned and stuck out his left arm that ended in a tin cup. A baby powder of snow was already gathering on the bill of his hat. "Just a di..."

"Get that away..." Randuzzi barked and swatted the old man's arm away. The empty cup fell, clattering, to the sidewalk near the gangster's left foot.

"Oh dear," said The Admiral his eyebrows painted white with snow. "Please accept my apologies. If you could kindly help me by just picking up my cup..."

"Get out of here before I slice you like a bologna, you damn fool!"

"Yes, yes, of course. But, you see, I can leave much faster if you'd retrieve my cup. You see, I'm blind..."

"Oh, for the love of God," said Randuzzi, and bent at the waist to pick up the cup.

"Yes," said The Admiral, "for the love of God," and raised his cudgel and smashed it down on the back of Randuzzi's skull.

Randuzzi fell to the snow-dusted sidewalk like a sack of wet flour, and lay still.

"Oh, dear," said The Admiral, "I do believe I've dropped my cudgel as well!"

So saying, he pulled a long, thin whistle attached by a string around his neck from beneath his suit coat, and blew on it.

It was then that a nest of vipers—Hank Catchem, Typhoid Mary, and Ham, with Jack Flash bringing up the rear on his platform—slid silently around the left corner of the slaughterhouse except for the erk erk erk of the wheels of Jack's platform, all headed for The Admiral.

Hank was the first to arrive at the old black man's side.

"Man," he said, "that was a lot easier than I thought it'd be; good job, Bridges."

"I still wish she'd let us bring guns," said Ham as he joined the two men. He patted the iron pipe held in his right hand into the open palm of his left hand. "This baby is great for close work, but not so great for long distance."

"Can't be a viper and kill a man," said Typhoid Mary on arrival. She raised her left fist tricked out with a pair of brass knuckles. She kidded the brass knuckles. "These are enough for me. You know the rules."

"Well, I'm glad you're all here anyway," said The Admiral. "Arguing as usual."

He extended his right arm and the cudgel he held towards the warehouse's door.

"Let me, let me, let me! Please?"

Without looking down to the source of the voice at his knees, Admiral James Bridges smiled.

"Go ahead, Jack, knock. Remember, we have the advantage of the element of surprise, my little friend."

With madness burning in his eyes, Jack raised his oar triumphantly and rapped on the door three times.

"Surprise!" he whispered.

Giovanni's prosthetic fist smashed the arm of the chair!

Leo Rosenbaum did not cry out or even flinch because his arms were safely bound behind the chair. The constant beatings by DeSalvio's thugs since his capture had left him emotionally dead, oblivious to pain, as well as blinded from the blood in his eyes. His battered head tipped partially towards his right shoulder, Leo's overcoat had been pulled halfway down his shoulders to initially pin his arms as well, and the ropes that tied his legs to the chair's legs had rubbed the flesh on his shins under his pants raw.

The two men with rifles guarding the entrance to the abandoned slaughterhouse watched a scene that they'd seen played out many times before as The Hammer stepped back from the shattered arm of the chair, raised his prosthetic, flesh colored, right hand clinched forever in a fist to the level of his face. Carlos Valentine, one step behind him and to his left, took a step back at the same time as his boss.

Four of The Hammer's henchmen, each wearing a shoulder holster, glanced up from the card table at which they sat, then turned eyes cold and indifferent back to their poker hands. Two of his thugs seated on a worn-out leather couch next to a wall—one reading a magazine and one cleaning his fingernails with a pocket knife—seemed oblivious to their boss, Carlos, or Leo.

"Let me knock his teeth down his throat," said Valentine as he stepped forward. He was also wearing a shoulder holster over a long-sleeved shirt. There were half-moons of sweat under each arm.

"You had your chance, Carlos," said Giovanni. "Sit down and shut up."

Valentine grunted his disappointment, found a folding chair leaning against the couch, and sat down and shut up.

"I reluctantly, and with some surprise, have to give you credit, Mr. Rosenbaum," The Hammer said, as he unbuttoned the buttons on the back of the thin, flesh colored glove on his upturned fist with his left hand. "My boys have had a lot of experience... extracting...information from unwilling men and women. You've held up much longer than I would have imagined for a gutless newspaper reporter."

Giovanni swept his fist around the large, mostly empty main room of the dilapidated building ringed with multi-paned windows that were so dirty that they were opaque. His grand gesture included the eight murderers, thieves, rapists, and flunkies that were the DeSalvio family at the moment.

"My boys have done most of their questioning in this very room. Seemed appropriate for an old slaughterhouse, eh, Rosenbaum? Because you've lasted this long, I am forced to ratchet it up a notch, so to speak, because of your reticence. Because you *will* tell me where I can find that leather-bound maniac you call Snake. Sooner or later. One way or another."

Leo shook the blood from his eyes and watched Giovanni peel the flesh colored glove off of his fist and let it dangle, limp, in front of the reporter's face.

"Here's a scoop you'll never report. Outside of my boys, you are the only man alive who has seen the iron fist under the flesh colored glove I always wear. Treasure your special moment. It won't last long. I show it to you so that you can keep what is going to happen in context. This is the hand that I used to crush the arm of your chair. It is the same hand I'll use to crush your face if you don't give it up, now."

Leo said nothing.

Giovanni took a step closer to the reporter.

"We are both reasonable, educated men, Mr. Rosenbaum. You must not think that I won't kill you. You are expendable. We'll find your wife, eventually. Husbands tell their wives everything, so she'll give me the information I want if you aren't alive to do so. Or I'll find Snake in some other way.

"Let me make my situation perfectly clear before I break every bone in your face. Hell will freeze over before I let that lunatic dame in leather underwear undo what it took my father and I so long to build in the Bowery.

"My father was John DeSalvio, remember him? The same John DeSalvio who ran the Bowery for fifty years. He was a fighter by the time he was fourteen when he boxed professionally as a lightweight. He was a bouncer when he first met some of Gotham's criminal elite. Eventually, he ran his own gang with close ties to the Eastman Gang, fought and won gang wars for control of gambling and labor-slugging undertakings. He ended up owning a couple of Manhattan saloons like the *Folly* over on Fourteenth Street, the *Mandarin Cafe* in the 'Bloody Angle' of Doyers Street.

"I grew up in his shadow, Mr. Rosenbaum, and in the shadow of his buddies, 'Lil' Augie Pisana', 'The Boss Giuseppe Masseria' and capo in 'Lucky' Luciano's family. My father got a Mayor elected and served as an assemblyman himself. He seemed invincible. He was stabbed by the Humpty Jackson Gang and shot by the Five Points Gang, but he outlasted them all and died of natural causes.

"I plan on going out the same way. But not because of Snake."

The gangster stuck his face only inches away from Leo's bruised face, and began to draw his iron first slowly and painfully down Leo's left cheek.

"And not because of a punk like you. I could kill you now, but, on the other hand..." he began, and stopped.

"That's kind of funny, isn't it," he said, and shoved Leo's head to one side with his iron first. He stood up straight and looked at his right hand.

"On the other hand. This hand. With this hand, I could just beat you to death."

"Your father was a schmuck," whispered the reporter through swollen lips. "And you're nothing but the son of a schmuck."

From the clinching of Giovanni's jaw, the flaring of his nostrils, and the squinting of his eyes, Leo knew that The Hammer was struggling to control a volcano of hatred seething inside the kingpin.

"Look around you, Rosenbaum," The Hammer said through clenched teeth. "I've got one of my best men posted outside the entrance to his dump, and the two inside standing by the door will die before they let anyone in."

The Hammer turned to face the men playing cards at a small card table to the left of him. "Wave to Leo, boys! See that, Mr. Reporter? Any one of those men would die for me. So, who do you think is going to save you? The Calvary? The Lone Ranger? Little Orphan Annie? The police? The *Bowery* police. Ha! Annie has a better chance to find me than the cops. So..."

There were three sharp raps *crack crack crack* on the entrance to the slaughterhouse. Giovanni's two henchmen looked at him for instruction.

"What are you, stupid?" Giovanni snarled. "See what Randuzzi wants!"

One of the men guarding the door opened it.

"Surprise!" Typhoid Mary, Ham, Hank, and Alfonso Longfellow yelled in the open door with their hands raised and fingers splayed.

"More surprise!" said Jack Flash.

Both guards followed Jack's voice down to see him grinning broadly, holding his oar on his shoulder like a baseball bat.

Jack swung the oar and struck the guard to his left in the groin with its blade. Then Jack swung his oar to the right and struck the guard there in the groin.

They both crumpled to the floor, moaning and clutching their injuries.

At the same instant, Snake smashed through a window in a hail of glass.

Giovanni turned to the startling sound of shattering glass behind him.

Snake landed, crouching on her left knee and the fingertips of her right hand, in a halo of shattered glass on the floor of the slaughterhouse.

She snapped her whip that she'd used like a rope free from its unseen anchor outside of the window and slowly raised her face from her chest.

Her eyes never leaving Giovanni, Snake slowly coiled her whip into a multilayered loop.

And hissed, "Let's dance!"

"What, no pat down?" asked Jack as he pushed himself into the slaughterhouse with his oar between the two DeSalvio guards cringing where they lay in fetal positions on the floor.

"At least they had a lot on the ball," said Alfonzo Longfellow as he straightened the lapel of his tuxedo and tails and stepped with dignity over one of Jack's victims.

"At least, at least," Jack repeated as he raised the shaft of his oar and struck the skull of the first of the two guards. He spasmed and lay still.

"On the ol' ball," Jack added, as he hit the second thug.

Then all Hell broke loose.

Typhoid Mary tailgated Jack. She scooped up the rifles of the two unconscious guards as Ham split away to her left side and Hank and Longfellow to her right side.

As they passed her, Typhoid tossed the rifles out the door.

"Two, two, two thugs in one!" she mugged.

She nodded at The Admiral still standing outside with his collar pulled up over his neck against the snow. He gave her a thumbs-up approval.

Scattering playing cards and chairs, the four men at the card table jumped to their feet, shouting. The two DeSalvio thugs sitting on the couch leapt to their feet.

Then the slaughterhouse became a raucous cacophony of striking, pounding, and slapping, the thud of iron and bone and flesh on flesh, the jarring sound of breaking furniture and glass, accented by the scraping of shoes, grunts of exertion, and the staccato yelps of men and women battling for life.

"Carlos!" Giovanni yelled.

His torpedo leapt from his chair and hurtled like a quarterback at Snake.

"You can't step in the same river twice," she said and threw back her head, laughed, and deftly sidestepped the thug, striking the back of his skull with her right elbow as he hurtled past her.

Thrown off balance, Carlos stumbled forward and fell on his face on the concrete floor with a flesh scraping, bone-jarring impact as Snake spotted two DeSalvio henchmen attacking Ham several yards away. One was drawing on them his revolver from his shoulder holster.

Snake cartwheeled across the concrete floor. A gun somewhere barked. She stopped, standing on her feet.

Snake leveled her right arm and pressed the flat pad in her palm with two fingers. Her dart hurtled true to bite the back of the gunman's neck. He slapped at it, cursing, then slumped to the floor.

Ham raised his left hand and its thumb, indicating thanks, as he swung his pipe back. Then the bouncer tapped the crown of the skull of his adversary who crumpled like paper to the floor.

"Next?" he grinned and, lifting a lamp off of an end table, smashed it on the floor. "I'm hot tonight!"

Her right arm still extended, the vigilante swiveled back to see Carlos struggling to his feet and drawing his gun from his shoulder holster.

"The calamity that comes is never the one we had prepared ourselves for," she said, and added, "Alley Oop!"

She pressed the flat pad in her palm.

The dart thudded into Carlos' chest. He staggered back a step, looking down at his chest as he did so. He looked up at Snake.

"Not this time" he bellowed and plucked the dart from his chest. He sneered as he let the dart fall it the floor. "Bullet-proof vest."

"Typhoid!" said one a DeSalvio's hoods as he began to snatch his gun from its holster. "What are you doin' here?"

As quick as a heartbeat, the madam swung a savage left full of brass knuckles up from her hip and under the hood's chin. He stumbled back as she followed and a second DeSalvio thug followed behind her, his gun drawn.

"I think it's called an uppercut, sugar," said Mary as she threw a second terrible fist of brass knuckles like a pile-driver into his stubbled face. He fell to the floor with a heavy grunt.

"And you're banned from the house for a week, too, sweetie," she added. "No hard feelings. Who's up for a knuckle sandwich?"

The heavy blow on the back of her skull nearly knocked her off of her feet.

She spun on her heels and threw back her left fist as she confronted her attacker.

"That hurt!" she spat. "Don't you know ya ain't supposed ta hit a lady, ya dope? Or a steam roller?"

Typhoid kicked him in the groin. He doubled over, clutching his injury, and fell to his knees in front of her. She knelt by his side and raised her brass knuckled left fist.

"And they were two of my best customers!"

Her fist swung. Another gunman yelped somewhere in the slaughterhouse.

At that moment, as Snake marched to Valentine with a deadly

determination in her step, Giovanni's torpedo snatched his revolver from its holster and slowly pointed it at Snake's heart.

"I said..." his voice cold dead, "not...this...time."

"Wanna bet?" she said, and snapped her whip from her hip. "I take my only exercise acting as a pallbearer at the funerals of my friends who exercise regularly. But, then again, you aren't my friend, Carlos Valentine."

Lashing her blacksnake whip back, Snake snapped it forward, biting Valentine's gun from his stung hand. "Let's see the Lone Ranger do that!"

"Damn it!" he yelled and grabbed the thong of the whip in his uninjured hand and yanked it towards him. His gun spun across the floor and out of his reach.

Alfonso Longfellow reached the couch before the first of the two gangsters was fully on his feet but with his gun drawn.

"Wait, sir, wait!" Longfellow said, presenting his upraised hands, palms forward. "I am no pugilist sir, I am a magician! Look!"

He lowered his arms, and pulled up the frayed left sleeve of his tuxedo with the thumb and index finger of his right hand. The thug was fully on his feet now.

"Nothing up this sleeve!" He grinned broadly as he began to pull up his right sleeve with the fingers of his left hand.

"And look! Nothing up this...."

Playing cards exploded into the crook's startled face.

"Oops!" grinned the magician.

The DeSalvio crony raised both of his hands up to protect his face. Longfellow snatched the gun from his right hand, dropped it on the floor, kicked it away, and punched the thug in the face with his left fist. The thug fell backwards over the arm of the couch to the floor.

"Well, I'm be damned," he grinned, "I guess I *am* a pugilist! Let's see if I'm a kick-boxer as well."

The magician seized both of the second thug's arms as he struggled to get off of the couch, pulled him up to his feet.

"Rise and shine," said Longfellow and kicked him in the groin.

"I learned that from the guy with the oar," grinned Longfellow.

Then he began to repeatedly kick the downed gangster in the stomach as he coolly checked the fingernail of his left hand and sang.

"Row, row, row your boat, gently down the stream..."

Jerked off balance, Snake released the whip and snatched her quarter-staff off of her back as she padded like a leopard towards Carlos.

"Touché," she hissed. "Let's see if you can play pick-up-sticks."

Valentine dropped the limp thong and pulled a knife from its hidden sheath beneath his left sleeve at the forearm and crouched.

"I'm going to cut you like a cheap whore," he rumbled and lunged, swiping a large arc with the knife as Snake side-stepped, raised her quarterstaff, and brought it down with bone-crunching force on his right forearm.

His knife flew out of his hand, spinning across the floor as he grabbed his right forearm and winched with pain.

"Damn it, damn it, damn it to Hell!" he yelped and viciously lunged.

Snake swung her quarterstaff, striking the right side of his head.

Valentine stumbled back and shook his head. Dazed, he swayed on his unsteady feet as blood began to trickle down his right ear. He raised his left hand to that ear, then looked at the smeared blood on its fingertips.

"But, you're just a woman," he muttered. "A woman. A damn skirt."

Hatred and shame burning in his eyes, Valentine shifted his weight from his left to his right foot like a boxer preparing for his final onslaught.

It was then that he saw Giovanni inching his way to a side exit.

At that moment, Jack Flash rolled up to a DeSalvio gangster and raised his oar to strike. The thug grabbed Jack's oar with both hands and struggled terrifically for its possession, almost lifting the double amputee off of his platform. When that didn't work, he shoved back on the oar with all of his strength. Jack and his platform began spinning backwards, but Flash slammed his hand down on the toggle switch for the brake to stop it from hitting a wall.

Jack yelled, "Flabgabbit!" then flipped the toggle switch to free the brake and began to furiously row back to his opponent.

The gangster firmly planted his feet on the floor and pulled his revolver. He leveled it at the Korean veteran's face.

He fired. The bullet whizzed by Jack's head.

Jack jammed his oar between the thug's legs, and twisted.

The thug fell hard, striking the floor.

Instantly, Jack was at his head, raised his oar over his head, and, with one mighty downward swing, clubbed the gangster unconscious.

The legless veteran then planted his oar on DeSalvio's flunkie like a flag on a mountain peak and yelled, "Excelsior!"

Ten feet away, Valentine watched Snake mirror his stance as he said, "Then I'll just beat you to death with my fists!" and lunged.

Holding her quarterstaff horizontally in front of her at her knees, Snake met his lunge with a powerful upward thrust that struck him beneath his chin and lifted the thug off of his feet.

Valentine back fell to the floor, bleeding from his mouth.

Snake walked to his side to stand over the unconscious thug.

"It's fun being in the same decade with you," she hissed. "Now, up, up and away!"

The vigilante then turned her back on Valentine and began to search the chaos of flailing arms and clashing bodies in front of her, but could not find Giovanni until her eyes fell on a side door of the slaughterhouse and watched the Hammer running into a column of snow blowing through it into the room.

Then, as graceful and silently as a leopard running on the balls of its feet, she scooped up her whip as she trotted after the mobster.

Quoting Roosevelt as she ran, she said, "There is nothing I love more than a good fight," and ran out into the snowstorm.

Snake stepped through the side door of the slaughterhouse into the nighttime eddies and currents of a surging, ocean of snow and the low roar of a heavy wind. She thought, *dart worthless,* because of the storm.

Snake tried but could not find Giovanni by the hazy halo of light around a single streetlamp at the entrance to or exit from what she guessed was an alley. Adding to her dilemma, the alley was littered with the blurred ghosts of trash cans, discarded equipment, and wooden crates and boxes stacked against both walls. So she chose to turn left, reasoning that the mouth of the alley would be DeSalvio's goal and that it would logically be located on the same side as the entrance to the abandoned slaughterhouse. She squinted into the dark as she first leaned into the driven snow, then stepped out into the torrent, and then began to trot, wiping the snow from the eye slits in her mask.

It was only a moment before the vigilante was able to find the receding ghost of DeSalvio's back not fifteen feet in front of her. She carefully picked up speed as she ran, removing her whip as she did so.

Snake redoubled her pace until only ten feet separated her from the mobster when she let the thong of her whip fall and trail behind her in the snow.

Eight, seven, six feet remained between them when she raised the thong and snapped it forward.

"Now, up, up, and away!"

In an instant, it wrapped and jerked taut around Giovanni's left calf in mid step.

She jerked the blacksnake whip back!

"Wha..?"

The Hammer sputtered and staggered as he was jerked around by the whip.

His forward momentum threw him backwards on the street where he fell, hard, on his butt.

And the revolver that he gripped in his left hand discharged in the frigid air.

At the entrance to the slaughterhouse, the Admiral looked up at the sharp report of a gunshot. He was trying to light a cigarette with a match cupped in a hand. He threw the lit match into the snow with the cigarette as he stumbled towards the sound.

A horizontal pile-driver of boot and rigid, extended legs, Snake leapt through the air and rammed into the mobster's chest where he sat, instantly knocking him flat on the concrete in the snow. Now straddling his chest and pinning both his arms to the street with her knees, she began to rapidly punch him with hard, staccato jabs, once, twice, three times in the face. Each punch earned a grunt of pain as his head was thrown side to side by the impact.

Suddenly, the vigilante released Giovano's left arm to snatch his gun from his left hand. Cursing through torn lips, Giovanni arched his back and Snake toppled off of him, rolled three times, and stopped, crouched on one knee in the deepening snow.

Gritting his teeth and cursing, The Hammer spat blood on the snow, then turned on his side towards her, raised himself on his right elbow, and leveled his gun squarely at Snake's chest.

He fired.

In mid-step, the Admiral looked up at the sharp report of the gun shot, and redoubled his speed.

"Oh," Snake gasped in a tiny voice as she jerked back and to her right side.

She reached up and clutched her right shoulder with her left hand.

Blood began to seep through scaled leather between her fingers.

She staggered up straight and took a step towards Giovanni.

"Oh," she said again, stopped and snatched her quarterstaff from its holster on her back with her left hand.

Disoriented and weakened by the pain, she fell down hard on her knees in the snow, her snake-headed quarterstaff across her thighs, breathing heavily.

Using his right arm and its metal hand to steady himself, the Hammer stood up with some difficulty and stumbled to Snake's side, his gun still leveled at her.

He placed its cold muzzle against her left temple.

"It's been a pleasure killing you," he snarled, and cocked the gun.

She did not raise her head.

She said, "The reports of my death have been greatly exaggerated."

Then she rammed her staff up.

His gun flew out of his hand and his chin jerked back and up. The gun spun away to disappear in the snow.

Cursing, The Hammer toppled back against a tall stack of wooden crates. He leveled his gun at her again, only to realize that he had lost it.

"Check..." Snake hissed, "...and mate," and wiped snow from the eye slits of her Kabuki mask.

"My ass," Giovanni gasped, stepped to the side of stacked wooden crates, and shoved them over.

The rain of crates fell in a riot of jagged shards and broken slats short and to one side of the leather-clad she-devil as she staggered to her feet.

"That was a cliché when your mother was still working at Typhoid Mary's house of whores," hissed Snake.

"Enough?" she managed to add through clenched teeth and raised her quarterstaff horizontally, defensively, across her chest.

Giovanni lunged.

A raving animal, his right hand was raised over his head like an axe.

The 'axe' swept down in a savage arc.

His iron hand snapped her quarterstaff in half, knocking it from Snake's now almost useless right hand.

Then Giovanni smashed her in the face with his metal fist, cracking her Kabuki mask from its left cheek to the point of its chin.

She fell, dazed, at the gangster's feet, moaning, unmoving.

The Hammer stood over her, unsteady on his feet, blood seeping from the corner of his mouth and his right ear.

The head of the DeSalvio crime family looked down at the woman that he hated with all of his being for a long moment. Then he stepped over her body with his left leg, straddling her.

He fell to the street, his knees straddling her chest, his butt slamming into her stomach, knocking her breath out.

He snatched the broken shard of her quarterstaff from her right hand.

Her eyes opened behind her Kabuki mask.

Clutching its ends with both hands, he thrust the length of the quarterstaff fragment across her throat and slowly began choking the vigilante.

"Kiss me, lover," she gasped as she cupped his chin and cheek with her left hand.

She pressed the pad in the palm of her hand hard against his jaw.

There was an inaudible *whit* and the dart buried itself deep in his throat.

Giovanni sat up, startled but unable to cry out, confused, his eyes dilated with fear, and swatted at the tail of the dart, trying to find and pull it out.

Suddenly, Giovanni's body went rigid.

Tiny bubbles, pink with blood, foamed at the left corner of his mouth.

Then Giovanni "The Hammer" DeSalvio, the vicious head of the DeSalvio crime family who ruled the Bowery with an iron hand, toppled off of Snake's chest and fell face down in the snow on the street.

Snake lay for long moments gasping for air on her back in the blowing snow before she was able to raise herself on her left elbow. She looked to her right side at the gangster lying paralyzed on the street, and shuddered. She looked to her left side and saw a ghostly figure approaching her, but still at some distance. Then Snake struggled to her feet next to Giovanni, breathing heavily.

She said, "Remember, you are just an extra in everyone else's play."

She nudged his side with her boot. He did not move.

Quoting Winston Churchill, she added, "Now this is not the end."

She placed her boot on his side and pushed his body over with some effort onto his back. Giovanni groaned but did not open his eyes.

She removed one of her cobra playing cards from an interior pocket at her waist and placed it carefully, half of the card showing, in his suit pocket.

"You'll be alright in the morning, tough guy. Might have to switch to menthol fags in prision, though. Don't forget to give that card to Lieutenant Manning." She said. "He's expecting you."

The Admiral arrived at her side.

"Are you alright?" he asked.

"This is not even the beginning of the end," she continued as if the Admiral hadn't spoken to her. "But it is, perhaps, the end of the beginning."

It was very early in the morning and very cold when Lieutenant Manning stood at the same window that Snake had used to enter his office on the third floor. Snow was still gathered in its outside lower corners. His hands were clutched behind him as a '42 Plymouth DeSoto that had been a bright green at one time and was obviously originally painted in a solid yellow, lurched to the curb in front of the Bowery's ninth precinct. It now looked like it was painted with dried mud. It was not wholly unexpected, so he watched, but did not react, as the driver and a huge man from the backseat jumped out of the taxi and trotted around it to its trunk.

"Well, I'll be damned," he muttered to himself, but without surprise.

The overcast sky was still spitting occasional, fat snow flakes. The trunk opened, and the two men lifted a gagged man who was not resisting and was heavily bound at the hands, feet, and knees with rope. That meant the bound man was either unconscious or dead. As they unceremoniously dumped him on a sidewalk covered with great dollops of snow, Manning could not be certain who the two men or the gagged man were because of his distance from them.

But he knew.

His policemen began to pour out of the building in twos and threes as the mystery men jumped back in the taxi and the vehicle sped away from the curb. Several service revolvers were pulled, there was a lot of gesturing, and one policeman scratched his head from a failed attempt to write down the numbers of its license plate. Words were spoken that Manning could not and did not need to hear to understand. Then one of his men ran full tilt back into the precinct building.

Manning made sure that the window was unlocked by testing its latch, then turned from it to patiently rock back and forth on the balls and heels of his well-polished shoes, watching the door.

The door exploded inward, and the policeman standing in the entrance and gasping for breath immediately saw him and blurted out, "Lieutenant Manning!

"It's the Hammer!"

Chapter Sixteen

October 1952, Bowery, New York City

"**W**hat's going on here, Hank?" asked Dr. Eacobacci as he looked out of the back window of the Star taxi cab. "First, I don't get blindfolded, then you don't keep that window that always separates us up, and now this? This looks like a flop house."

"You sure do ask a lot of questions, doc," said Hank, adjusting the dial of his radio to stop on Percy Faith's "Delicado". He looked up at Eacobacci framed in his rear-view mirror. "You'd think that a shrink would have just a little bit of patience, you know. We're at 241 Bowery, the Sunshine Hotel, just like the sign says, and that's all you need to know right now. So you need to get out of my taxi and go into the hotel. All your answers are in there, bud. Now get."

Eacobacci squeezed his massive frame out of the door of the taxi to stand on the edge of the curb of a sidewalk covered with snow that the foot traffic had churned into a dirty mush. He looked up at the dilapidated Sunshine Hotel as the taxi pulled away from the curb. Then he checked to make sure that his rolled up newspaper was tucked firmly under his left arm. It was there.

The building wasn't much different than the sidewalk—three stories of dirty mush with its name written in neon on a sign perpendicular to the building just above the entrance, a rusty fire-escape that zigzagged to its highest floor and a series of multi-paned windows set in crumbling brick on the second and third floors. The psychologist took off the Fedora that had replaced his typical pair of sunglasses, and beat it against his great coat, dusting off imaginary dirt.

"What the Hell," he muttered to a sidewalk sparsely populated with men and a few women hunched over because of the cold, and walked up to the door. He pushed it open, and stepped inside.

As he entered, a man behind a metal mesh window to his left glanced up and then back down to finish whatever he had been doing. His unshaven face, dirty hair, and heavy dollops of flesh beneath his eyes did nothing to win him favor with Eacobacci. The flophouse's manager or cashier looked little different from the other skid-row bums—the flotsam of society—scattered around the small lobby, slumped on chairs or worn sofas along the walls or at cheap card tables in dirty under- or third-hand shirts and worn, shiny trousers. It was a depressing scene, even for the upbeat psychologist.

The lobby and the men smelled like urine, booze, and illness.

"Is that you, Doctor Eacobacci," said a voice without a body.

The psychologist searched for and found the voice. The Admiral sat on a raunchy couch by a wall to his right that was so close that Eacobacci had overlooked it. As always, he was dressed in a second-hand, wrinkled suit that had once been black and creased, cuffed pants. Eacobacci's principal contact with Snake was wearing sun glasses, his close-cropped hair was peppered with gray, his mustache was unevenly trimmed, and he was sitting as if he wer oblivious that the door was open.

James Bridges stood up and extended a hand in the wrong direction to be shaken.

"I've been expecting you, doctor," said the wizened old man. "Please," he added and turned his extended hand palm up as if expecting help. "That door directly across the lobby from where you are probably standing is where we need to go."

The psychologist came to the old black man and took his hand. As they moved towards the so indicated door, he couldn't help but notice that the black man did not smell of booze and urine.

"What is this all about, Admiral. Every little routine connected with my meeting with Snake has been broken today."

"That," answered The Admiral, "is because today is a hap, hap, happy day, doc. Today, you're going to meet the grand lady of a nest of vipers in her nest."

"In her..." Eacobacci began, but deeper consideration killed his remaining words as they moved down a claustrophobic hallway.

"You'll notice the rows of little, four-by six foot cubicles we're passing, doc," said the Admiral as they maneuvered down the hall. "We call them 'pigeon coops'—just enough room for a little mattress and a few personal possessions."

He stopped the psychologist with an outstretched arm.

"We're here," he said, and opened a door that swung out into the hall.

Eacobacci saw that his guide had not exaggerated. There was barely enough room for a small man to stand up or to move around the cheap mattress on its floor, or to avoid colliding with the clothing hanging from both its walls and ceiling.

"Please," said Bridges as he sat down on the edge of the mattress. "Sit down."

Having no real alternative, the psychologist sat down next to the Admiral on the edge of the mattress.

"Prepare yourself for a surprise," said James Bridges, and pushed something hidden on the wall.

The bed began to sink.

Eacobacci gripped the edge of the mattress and said, "What's happening!?"

"You will receive a great honor in just a few moments, doctor. You have been invited to Snake's personal apartment."

"I'm not sure I was given an option," said the psychologist as the floor of the cubicle and its mattress continued to slowly sink. "How many people know about this?"

"Just the nest, and now you, doc. Snake's Nest of Vipers."

As it sank, bits of objects and walls slowly revealed themselves until Eacobacci was certain that the elevator was descending into a fully furnished apartment.

The mock pigeon hole/service elevator finally jerked to a stop on the floor of an apartment that carried its own surprises. It was a basement that nevertheless bore all the furnishings of wealth.

Against a wall papered with rich floral designs to the right of where the Admiral and the psychologist sat was a chest-of-drawers, and on it, an ornate, iron, Art Deco picture frame and a photograph of two little girls—all pony tails, ribbons, and smiles. On the wall behind the chest-of-drawers was mounted a grouping of four, Chinese masks made of porcelain—a laughing blue Kabuki mask, a yellow Kabuki mask of fear, a blue one of sorrow, and a white Kabuki mask of indifference—a Kabuki mask identical to the one Snake wore when in full regalia.

Next to the chest-of-drawers, a small phonograph player rested; its dark, cherry-wood lid opened with a record ready to play on its turntable.

Against the wall to the left of the men who were now rising from the mattress, stood an upright piano. At it sat Alfonso Longfellow dressed like a cheap burlesque magician in a tattered suit with tails and a top hat, his slender fingers gliding over the keys. The melancholy chords of Beethoven's *Für Elise* swelled up and filled the apartment. Longfellow nodded his approval of their arrival and smiled as the Admiral and Ecobacci stepped off of the service elevator.

Opposite the two men stood an overstuffed chair next to a large couch. Smoking a fat cigar, Typhoid Mary waved her greeting from the chair.

Next to her, a tortoise-shell cat lay curled on a couch by Snake who wore a luxuriant, white, terry-cloth robe cinched at the waist, a sling supporting her right arm, and her cracked Kabuki mask.

"Welcome to the nest," said the leather-clad she-devil. "I'm glad you could come."

"I'm glad that one of us can say that with a straight face," answered Ecobacci as he approached the couch. Typhoid Mary stood up.

"Please, doc," said Typhoid, "sit here."

"Thank you, but I think I'll stand."

"Thank you too, doc," said Typhoid in a tone that broached no disagreement, "but you'll sit."

Ecobacci sat down.

"I see that you are wearing a sling," said the doctor, and removed the newspaper from beneath his arm and opened it. He held it up. The headline read:

SNAKE NAILS THE HAMMER
Kidnapped Zhurnal Reporter Released

"Old news is no news, Doctor Eacobacci," said Snake.

"True, but it is why I'm here today. I have come to say goodbye."

"For goodness sake, why?"

"As is made obvious by the headline," said the psychologist, lowering the newspaper, "our sessions together have done you no good whatsoever."

"On the contrary, they have done me a world of good! Ask yourself this: why no blindfold today? Why is our meeting place no longer a secret and is, in fact, my very apartment? I will answer for you. Today, I will reveal my soul to you. And, in return, you will soon become the personal psychologist to Giovanni 'The Hammer' DeSalvio while he rots in jail. And you will feed me all of the information you learn from him about the mob in the Bowery and in New York City.

"Today, my dear doctor, you have joined my Nest of Vipers."

"I will do nothing of the sort," said Ecobacci as it struck him like a ton of bricks that Snake was not responding with non-sequitors nor speaking in quotes.

"I, in return, will take off my mask."

The chords from the piano stopped and the silence became palpable as, one by one, each of the Nest of Vipers turned to face the doctor and Snake.

The psychologist sat speechless as well.

"Didn't you say it would be one of the first steps to my recovery, Doctor Eacobacci? Didn't you tell me that I can never escape my demons until I reveal my name, remove my mask, and speak with absolute candor? Here is the candor.

"You would not recognize my given name," Snake continued as she lifted the lower edge of her Kabuki mask at her chin, "therefore, my name is unimportant.

"Why do I wear this mask? I was captured, imprisoned and tortured in Berlin in the final days of the war," she said. "I can never appear in public again because my face was...horribly, terribly, irreparably...mutilated."

So saying, she stripped off the mask.

She had large, deep blue, penetrating eyes, high cheek bones, flawless almond skin, full lips, and a heart-shaped jaw. Her brown hair, no longer bleached blonde, cascaded to her shoulders.

With her voice no longer distorted by her mask, she said:

"I am Snake."

It was the face of Amy Smith.

Dr. Eacobacci closed and locked the door to his office.

He walked deliberately to his desk and sat down.

His hand trembling, the psychologist picked up the handset of his telephone, dialed a number, and leaned back in his tufted, brown leather chair behind his well-organized mahogany desk. Behind him, a large, plate-glass window gave him a wonderful view of the skyscrapers of the Big Apple.

As the telephone rang, he looked at the little wooden bird at the right side and front edge of his desk that dipped its beak into a shot-glass full of water, then slowly jerked up, bobbed, then dipped again. Someone picked up the handset of the telephone on the other end of the line.

"Hello?" said Eacobacci.

"Hello," answered the gruff, male voice on the other line of the telephone. "Ninth Precinct. How can I help you?'

"This is Doctor...Doolitle. May I speak with Lieutenant Sam Manning?"

"Hold, please," the bird dipped.

Eacobacci tapped his finger on the casing on the telephone's mouthpiece as he waited impatiently. The bird rose, then bobbed.

"Hello, this is Lieutenant Manning. How may I help you?"

Eacobacci abruptly placed his hand over the bird. It stopped dipping.

"Hello Lew. I thought you might want to know.

"I've stumbled onto a nest of vipers."

October 1952, Bowery, New York City

It was unseasonably warm when Snake stepped out of the little wooden shed that protected the stairwell onto the middle of the roof of the Sunshine Hotel. The dollops of snow on the roof sculpted into other shapes by the objects they covered were slowly melting under a clear, blue sky.

She wore her leather fighting togs and her mask with the exception of her hydraulic dart gun.

As was always true, Snake started her regimen by stretching her arms to touch the sky, then lowering and stretching them behind her back, swinging them forward and bending her body to touch her toes with her fingertips.

She began to hum Beethoven's *Fifth Symphony* as she performed each movement with the grace of a tiger.

She performed a series lunges, one leg forward at a time, and ended her warm-up exercises with a quick series of squats.

She paused, took a deep breath, then raised her slender arms, her hands loose, and Plied several time with all of the grace and beauty of a ballerina performing for an adoring, imaginary audience. Seamlessly, she fell forward in a front split handstand position called a front walkover. Both of her booted feet were brought down, one after the other, towards her back. When her feet touched the roof, one after the other, her body followed. She repeated her walkover two more times.

Then she Plied again, spun around like a falling leaf, shook relaxation into the muscles of her body, and performed a backward flip, landing on her hands, her legs following together, ending the movement in a standing position.

Beethoven's rich, powerful orchestration now filled only her mind, and the scope and speed of her movements increased as she stepped first into an Arabesque and then ran a few steps, placed her dominant foot forward flat on the floor slightly away from her front foot and, with the leg behind, kicked off of the roof. Then she pushed her front leg off to land standing— a perfect front handspring.

Without hesitation, she broke without conscious effort into a Tendu of ballet, the product of years of dance lessons as a child. Then the formal, graceful movements of ballet morphed into ballroom dancing as she held and was held, held and released, held and was held by an imaginary Gene Kelly. She and Gene spun round an invisible couch on the roof like a whirlwind that ended as she threw herself forward and onto the floor, her knees tucked in as far as possible, in the rolling movement of a backward and, with a sudden flip, a forward somersault.

With the blood and Beethoven pounding in her heart, Snake again fell to the floor of the roof, her hands touching the roof one at a time, to her right side, her legs following in a cartwheel. From this, moving faster and faster, and seemingly without effort, she began to dance the East Coast Swag.

Now, without her hands touching the roof of the Sunshine, she performed an aerial cartwheel that broke into a wild, breathless Foxtrot.

Snake collapsed on the floor. After long moments, she stood, and raised her arms triumphantly for her invisible audience. Then she bowed twice at the waist.

Breathing deeply from her exertion, she moved to the ledge of the building facing Bowery Street and sat down.

She said, 'oh' and, suddenly, was overwhelmed with the memory of a Nazi spy, her face completely hidden by cotton bandages, sitting on a little metal stool with a mirror in her lap, and of the surgeon who had changed her life forever.

"I have done my best," his words replayed in her head. "I have tried to bring out the real you, darling."

"Thank you..." whispered Gretchen, and *Für Elise again* swelled to fill the tiny operating room.

"Sssssh. Don't try to talk now, sweetheart. It moves the wrappings."

Doctor Reigelmann snipped through another length of cotton swath and began to unwind it from her face.

"It's not unusual for a patient to be surprised and even disappointed initially, Gretchen. We all have a picture in our heads of how we ideally would like to look."

Max dropped a bandage scroll on the floor at his feet.

"We are almost done. There, and there. Your mirror is in your hands, dear."

Max stepped back and pulled a revolver from beneath his white smock.

"Take a moment to open your eyes. The light may initially blind you."

He took three clumsy steps back from where she sat on the chair in a little nest of white scrolls on the floor.

"An eye for an eye..." Max said, his voice shaking, and put the pudgy finger of his right hand through the trigger guard of his pistol. "I always knew, sweetheart. I tried to forget, but I couldn't."

"I didn't want it to happen this way." Tears streamed down his scarred and broken face, a face that had been beaten black and blue and lacerated by the Nazis, and his hand holding the revolver visibly shook.

"A tooth for a tooth," he said as his voice fell cold and dead and Max leveled the gun at Gretchen's face.

"When the Nazis were torturing me in Berlin, they told me it was you. That you betrayed me. That you killed Franz. That I was brutally tortured and condemned to a concentration camp because of you."

Oblivious to his words because of the rapture of anticipation of her new face, Gretchen began to open her eyes and raise the mirror.

"No," he exclaimed as the consequences of his work with scalpel and stitch and acid pushed its way up through his hatred and denial.

"No. What have I done?

Then the little hunchbacked dwarf turned the revolver on himself, placing the barrel of the gun on his right temple.

"Gretchen," he said and pulled the trigger.

And blew out his brains.

Gretchen lifted the mirror in front of her face.

Only one heard the staccato report of the revolver that sounded like a rim shot on a snare drum.

Only one heard Max's corpse hit the floor with a thud.

Only one heard Gretchen scream and scream and scream.

And then, as quickly as it had begun, her memories ended and Snake was on the roof of the Sunshine Hotel in the Bowery again. She looked down at a modestly expensive bracelet of precious stones inlaid in a low grade of gold that Max had given her and that she still wore on her right wrist.

Then she unhooked the thin, pink straps that ran around her head and beneath her hair and held her cracked, Kabuki mask in place.

She removed the mask.

She took off her wig and let it drop to the floor.

Her large, deep blue, penetrating eyes were all that remained of a face that had once stunned men.

She looked down at the concave inner surface of her Kabuki mask and wiped sweat from the mutilated flesh of her disfigured forehead and scalp with her right hand; from skin that, scarred forever by acid, was a horror of zigzagged, cracked flesh like parched desert sand.

Like the scales of a cobra.

She wiped sweat from the corners of a mouth that had been forever slit from cheek bone to cheek bone in that cracked face.

She wiped sweat from the gaping, black holes left from where her ears and nose had been cut off by Max's scalpel. And then she began to sob.

She wept for her sister who had been raped and murdered by the Nazis, and for herself, whom they had brutalized and beaten into submission, for the enemies of Hitler whom she had seduced and betrayed, for the hundreds of faceless victims of her betrayals that had been slaughtered on the battlefields and in the concentration camps of World War II because of the information she'd given to Hitler. She sobbed for what she had done to survive, and she cried for the only man whom she'd ever grown to love, Max Riegelmann.

When her broken heart held no more tears, she whispered in a voice no longer artificially distorted by her mask.

She whispered, "My name, my *real* name, doctor Eacobacci, is...Tzeitl.

"Tzeitl Katzenberger.

"But little Tzeitl is dead.

"Now and forever more....

She licked her lips with her forked tongue.

"I am Snake."

On the third floor rooftop of the building across the street from the Sunshine Hotel, a tall, bald man in an overcoat slowly lowered his field glasses. His expression was a mixture of shock and horror.

His name was Ben Alashee.

THE END

Richard E. Hughes

Comic book pioneer, writer, and editor, Richard E. Hughes, was a Mystery Man in the truest sense of that early term used to describe superheroes.

Some of that mystery is due to his use of pseudonyms—commonly used by artists, writers, and editors in the early days of the art form because the general population thought comic books were "kid stuff". In addition, they were not thought of as a serious art form by many who considered them just another passing fad in an industry where new magazines frequently appeared and disappeared from newsstands and candy stores. Therefore, bylines on stories were usually non-existent, sporadic, or even misleading.

Richard E. Hughes is infamous for using false names in the work produced by the Sangor shop and published by other companies starting in 1940, and by publisher B. W. Sangor's *American Comics Group* (ACG) from 1943 to 1967. Not only did this policy include Hughes' editorial use of pen names for his own writers and artists, even Richard E. Hughes was a pseudonym.

Additionally, Hughes' credit as a writer on specific ACG stories is still most often a mystery because records were not kept of much of the creative or business activity in the infant industry, and Hughes was no exception, adding to the enigma surrounding his own body of work.

However, it is known that Richard E. Hughes was born on November 5, 1909, and lived until January 15, 1974 when he died at the age of 65 of myeloribrosis, a rare blood disease.

Richard E. Hughes

It was the opinion of his wife and the artists and writers with whom he worked that Hughes was always impeccably and fashionably dressed, almost never found without his pipe in his mouth, enjoyed parties, loved to laugh (often at his own beloved puns) and was among the most kind, considerate, and professional editors in the business of comic books. It is also clear that Hughes and his wife, Annabel, were married on January 19, 1935—he was 26 years old — and their almost forty years of marriage produced only one famous offspring: the *American Comics Group*. Hughes worked there until 1967.

It is now also known that in 1942, when Hughes was 32 and his wife was 30 years old, they lived at 120 West 183rd Street in the Bronx, that he stood 5' 8" tall, weighed 170 lbs., and listed his occupation as editor. Annabel stood at 5' 4" in height, weighed 119 lbs., and listed no occupation. This personal information comes from their WWII war ration books, part of a large package of Annabel's personal possessions owned, at this writing, by a Yonkers, New York resident, Joseph Eacobacci. Joseph bought this amazing cache of materials from a former boyfriend of Annabelle's after her death and mailed this collection to the editor of *Alter Ego* magazine, Roy Thomas, for review and for identification. You met Joseph (he is not a psychologist!) in this novel, *Snake*.

The more than forty items in the Eacobacci collection included mostly black and white photographs from the 1930s not limited to the only known color photograph of the comics pioneer, manuscripts mostly typed on cheap newsprint intended for radio and television, as well as a comic strip proposal, multiple copies of two novels, a short story, and original greeting card verses. It also included more than a dozen printer's proofs of ACG covers, and two black and white advertisements that were meant for publication in an undesignated trade magazine. Among these proofs are three complete comic books stories of the "funny animal" variety.

Hughes was a pioneer in the comic book industry and was one of its most prolific and influential editors and writers during his lifetime. "Dick" created dozens of memorable characters, edited thousands of comic book stories, and most likely wrote well over a thousand of them in his career. Yet, when describing himself in his last resume, he wrote, "An experienced and competent editor...a writer who knows how to employ the right words. Public relations oriented. Expert in visual writing. Able to wed words and illustrations with maximum effectiveness."

Richard Hughes' career during the Great Depression of the 1930s is ignored in his resume. Only his graduation in 1930 at age 21 from New

York University with a Bachelor of Arts degree (English major, Economics minor) is recorded. On his résumé, he listed no occupation before 1940 (when he was 31 years old). Thereafter, for one year, he worked as a sales correspondent for Standard Mirror and Metal Products of New York City. He was involved in catalog production, including writing product copy. He left this position "to secure higher wages" at Syndicated Features Corporation in New York City in 1941.

In that year, Hughes edited and wrote a magazine of satire and comedy for publisher B.W. Sangor (1889-c.-1955) entitled *TNT*. It was a tabloid-sized magazine.

Eacobacci's collection includes pencil sketches for a "T.N.T." logo . It is not certain that the "T.N.T." logo was meant for use for the *TNT* magazine, although it seems probable that it was a new logo meant for the second issue.

Also in 1941, B. W. Sangor began publishing what remains a puzzling magazine that may have led to his entering the field of comic books. A rare copy of *Cinema Comics Herald* produced by the Sangor shop is part of the Eacobacci package. It is not certain that Hughes wrote or just edited these advertising comic books.

Cinema Comics Herald was a tiny, promotional comic book used at first to advertise Max Fleischer's animated *Mr. Bug Goes To Town* at movie theaters. *Cinema Comics Herald* was a movie theater giveaway.

By 1942, Hughes had become the best-selling writer and creator of The Black Terror, an early superhero who first appeared in *Exciting* and *America's Best* comic books, produced by the Sangor shop for pulp magazine publisher Ned Pines (1905-1990). Hughes had also created and was scripting two additional superheroes, The Fighting Yank and Pyroman, as well as The Commando Cubs and Super Mouse (the first super-animal slightly predating the super-mouse, Mighty Mouse), all solidly popular comic book features for the same publisher.

Richard Hughes' opportunity came as a result of being in the right place at the right time — New York City at the birth of a new art form. It was his talent, however, that secured him his position with Syndicated Features Corporation, one of the many branches of the Sangor shop. In the beginning, Hughes listed his position as an editorial assistant, with proofreading, newspaper correspondence, and advertising copy writing responsibilities. Still, the Sangor shop also produced finished art and stories for several comic book publishers, all hungry for material to sell to a growing audience.

Hughes' achievements in this new medium were not specifically mentioned on his resume, nor was it listed that he was writing and editing characters such as Doc Strange, Thunderhoof, American Eagle, and Supersleuths. In addition, he was editing a staggering number of other features while employed as a "proofreader". According to his résumé, these successes won him a promotion to the rank of editor at Syndicated Features in 1943. He named Sangor's company *The American Comics Group*, although it did not actually exist under that name until 1946. Now Hughes was both managing editor and business manager. He was not listed as editor in any title, however, until 1946, when the complicated and confusing handful of businesses owned by B.W. Sangor were all grouped together under the ACG insignia.

As a principal Sangor Shop editor, Hughes was writing and overseeing material not only for Pines but also for *DC Comics, Rural Home, LaSalle*, and *Leffingwell* publishers. His notes indicate that he was writing or editing The Phantom Stranger, Miss Masque, and dozens of lesser-known features at this time.

Not long after Hughes' named the comic book publishing side of Sangor's conglomerate of businesses *American Comics Group*, a postwar downturn in comic book sales, the threat posed by television and public concern over comic book content convinced Sangor to close down his shop (1948). Thereafter, Richard Hughes' principal efforts would be focused on expanding his little giant, ACG.

He began to broaden the titles released through the *American Comics Group*. Eventually, he would create, edit or write for 34 different ACG titles. In all, 1,010 comic book issues would be released by the end of 1967 (not including either *Custom Comics* or *Modern Comics* books). At ACG's peak, in 1952, Hughes edited and wrote for at least 16 titles. During his career with ACG, Richard helped create the first continuing horror series in comics, *Adventures into the Unknown*. He also created the characters of Herbie, Magicman, Nemesis, and (possibly) John Force, Magic Agent. The books *Herbie* and *Forbidden Worlds* won Alley Awards in 1964 as superior comics, and Hughes' patriotic stories even prompted a letter of thanks from the White House.

The success of the *American Comics Group* under Hughes' management led to a separate imprint, *Custom Comics*, also called *Culver Comics* (1954), which Hughes did not create. His résumé described *Custom* as an arm of ACG that produced "special purpose magazines for major commercial companies and governmental agencies. Purpose: public relations and sales promotions. Write major portion of such materials." Hughes did so through 1967, but copies dated as late as 1977 prove that *Custom Comics* remained a viable property even after his death and into the 1980's, as confirmed by then ACG final publisher Frederick Iger (1924—?). These comic books were produced for police and fire departments, Buster Brown Shoes, the U.S. Air Force, and dozens of other institutions; they were given away free or as product premiums.

Joseph Eacobacci's collection contains seventeen copies of these advertising booklets and one related trade magazine.

Advertising Requirements, the trade magazine in this collection, featured an article on comic books in its February, 1961 issue. That article includes facts about *Custom Comics* that are amazing. In it, the number of Buster Brown promotional comics is listed at 50 to 75 million. Yes, million. They had been produced since 1959 by *Custom Comics*. Hughes and his crew had produced 35 Wrangler Jeans promotional comics since 1957, totaling 45 million copies. These distribution numbers are staggering; outstripping the sales of any newsstand title, and Richard E. Hughes edited all of them, and wrote most of the books.

One of ACG's most popular comic book titles sold on magazine racks was *Herbie*, published for twenty-three issues from 1964 to 1967.

Then as now, it is a standard practice among publishers to produce stories well in advance of publication, and among the recently discovered ACG materials from Joseph Eacobacci were three unpublished Herbie manuscripts! Two were scheduled for the twenty-fourth issue of the title; one was scheduled for an earlier issue, but was not published.

So ends the adventures of one of Hughes' greatest creations. But the Eacobacci package first mailed to *Alter Ego* magazine editor Roy Thomas and then forwarded to me for identification of the materials added three additional mysteries to the life and work of Richard E. Hughes. We now know with certainty that he wrote and edited other non-comics related materials even with his amazing work load.

At some time in his career, Hughes wrote seven days of scripts with multiple pages of character development and suggestions for a syndicated, newspaper comic strip. It was to be drawn by artist and personal friend, Kurt Schaffenberger. It was called *Love Clinic*, and was based on the same premise as popular newspaper advice columns like *Dear Abby*. It was intended that readers would send in relationship problems seeking advice, and Hughes' characters would visually present solutions. It is unknown if the typed, double-spaced work was actually drawn and submitted to any syndicate, and is improbable that *Love Clinic* was ever published.

Wagon Train West proposed "a story line that packs colorful thrills

Kurt Schaffenberger and Richard E. Hughes

aplenty" in fourteen pages of typed, double-spaced script. There is no year on the synopsis or information on the manuscript of its intended medium, whether it was to be for comics, for a television show, a novel, or movie production, and the synopsis reads like the first installment of a proposed series.

During his career in comic books, Richard Hughes also wrote material meant for production in radio and television, and for publication in magazines or as novels.

Although it does not indicate the year it was written or the program it was written for, *Scream Forth Your Love* is a nine page science-fiction/horror play probably intended for a fifteen-minute radio show. It is unknown if this radio script was ever produced.

The only short story in the collection is titled *Quarter-Section*, and neither the year it was written nor the magazine it was submitted to are indicated on the manuscript. It is a nine page, "mainstream" story.

Most probably in July of 1968 when ACG was 'closing down', according to Hughes' cover letter (although the last issue of a newsstand comic book was released in 1967), Hughes submitted verse to the Norcross Greeting Card Company. Norcross is recognized as the first publisher of Valentine's Day cards. It is unknown at this time if Hughes' greeting card verses were accepted and published by Norcross.

Sales-Films was another division of the ACG conglomerate, and there are four scripts in Eacobacci's collection that advertise the benefits of buying *Reader's Digest* magazine. Although it is obvious from Hughes' directions in these two or three page scripts that they were meant to be filmed, it is impossible to determine their exact use. Certainly meant for possible subscribers, they are nevertheless too long for television commercials and too short for documentaries.

Another of Hughes' works in this collection is *Look Out for Celia*, a murder mystery, 107 page screenplay written in an unknown year for an undesignated market.

It is almost certain that Hughes did write at least two screenplays in the earliest days of television that were produced.

Valiant Lady was a fifteen minute long soap opera that was broadcast live from New York City by CBS television from October 12, 1953 through August 1957. One of the two manuscripts in this cache of Hughes materials is a 16 page screenplay for episode #36, run on Monday, November 30, 1953. Hughes' name is not on the manuscript; this episode is credited to the series' head writer, Charles Elwyn, a practice common at the time. But it is typed on the same cheap newsprint as all of Hughes' manuscripts, production notes on the cover page are detailed and specific, and the obvious question must be why would it be in Hughes' papers if he hadn't written it? His wife, Annabel, and Norman Fruman, who wrote for ACG and worked in their offices with Hughes, both mention his work on television. However, no screenplay work is mentioned on his resume.

It is almost certain that *Squeeze Play* was written by Hughes and aired on CBS television on May 12, 1953 as an episode of *Danger*. *Danger* was broadcast from 1950 to 1955 as a half-hour of "psychological dramas and murder mysteries" telecast from New York City on Tuesdays from 10:00 to 10:30 pm Eastern Standard Time. It also seems certain that the manuscript found in this collection is not complete, with a two page script example that reads "Half-Hour Continuity". The screenplay, credited to Alex Furth, is 7 pages in length with a theme of political blackmail and intrigue.

The Path of the Panther is Hughes' sixty page, detailed synopsis and two sample chapters for a novel that would be called a suspense thriller in today's market.

Despite several of his artists stating that Hughes was particularly sensitive and negative about any sexual innuendo in comic books, one of the principal themes in *The Path of the Panther* is lust. Several of the scenes are graphic in their description of foreplay, and profanity and violence are scattered throughout the synopsis and sample chapters.

Westchester Weekend is a full novel, also inexpensively bound, but typed on a higher quality of paper than what Hughes used for most of his other scripts.

Richard Hughes produced his last mainstream comic book work for *DC Comics* in 1967, writing uncredited stories for comic book titles including *Jimmy Olsen* and *Hawkman*, as well as for several mystery anthology titles. Giving Hughes credit for authoring those stories now is based on the best opinion of several comic historians who specialize in identifying writers and artists by their styles, as well as on the opinion of Hughes' widow.

Stranger yet is *Cobra*, a six page synopsis for a horror story that does not fit the standard format for comic books, television, or motion picture submissions at the time. It was too graphically gruesome for publication in an ACG horror or supernatural title, and uncharacteristic of the style popularized by EC horror comics. It is the basis for this novel, *Snake: Nest of Vipers,* and is published unedited in this volume.

Hughes ended his career and his life outside the art form of comics writing response letters to complaints for Gimbel's Department Store in New York City.

Richard Hughes created important super-heroes during the early history of comic books, as well as the first funny-animal parody of Superman. As the driving force behind the first horror comic book, he inadvertently helped spark the comic book witch hunt of the 1950s that almost destroyed the art form in America. The ACG title *Adventures into the Unknown* led to dozens and dozens of imitations, among them *EC Comics'* horror books, which are now thought by many critics to be the finest ever published. These EC titles inspired novelists like Stephen King and movie directors, including John Landis. In addition, many of the EC stories were adapted directly into movies and into a series on cable television, *The Vault of Horror.*

Hughes' *American Comics Group* was one of the few publishers to survive the Comics Code Authority that it helped initiate. His mark on the history of comics is indelible, and his career can never be duplicated. Hughes' life was important as "one of the best editors" in the so-called Golden and Silver Ages of comic books.

Even today, Richard Hughes is synonymous with the *American Comics Group* in the minds of thousands of comic book readers. This identification is so powerful that a long-enduring myth has grown, among fans and early comics historians alike, that Hughes wrote almost everything in every ACG title. This idea is amazing considering that his name never appeared on a cover, rarely on a letters page or as the host of a story, and never in the credits for any story. Indeed, his reputation continued to grow for years after the *American Comics Group* ceased publishing. Although personal name recognition was never used as a marketing tool by Hughes, his influence, editing, and writing touched every magazine containing material from the Sangor Shop or released under the ACG shield for more than twenty-

Richard E. Hughes

five years. And, as evidenced by their accomplishments with other publishers after having left ACG or the Sangor Shop, hundreds of artists and writers carried Hughes' influence, despite the mystery and enigma that surrounds much of his life, throughout the industry of three decades of the most popular art form on Earth — comics.

*Includes some material from Michael Vance's book, *Forbidden Adventures: The History of the American Comics Group*, and issues of *Alter Ego* magazine.

ABOUT OUR CREATORS

AUTHOR

MICHAEL VANCE - was born in Oklahoma City, Oklahoma. He was first published in *The Professor's Story Hour* chapbook at the age of eleven. He has been published in dozens of magazines and as a syndicated columnist and cartoonist in over 500 newspapers. His history book, *Forbidden Adventure, The History of the American Comics Group*, has been called a "benchmark in comics history". It was reprinted in *Alter Ego* magazine #s 62 & 62. His magazine work has been published in seven countries, and includes articles for *Starlog, Jack & Jill* and *Star Trek, The Next Generation*.

He briefly ghosted the internationally syndicated comic strip, *Alley Oop*, and created and wrote his own strip for five years called *Holiday Out* that was reprinted as a comic book. Vance also wrote comic book titles including *Straw Men, Angel of Death, The Adventures of Captain Nemo, Holiday Out* and *Bloodtide*. Artists with whom he has worked include Wayne Truman, Richard "Grass" Green, and Dave (*Alley Oop*) Graue. His work has appeared in several comic book anthologies, and he is listed in two reference works, the *Who's Who of American Comic Books* and *Comic Book Superstars*. His thirty short stories about a fictional town called "Light's End" have been published in numerous magazines. They have also been recorded by legendary actor William (*Murder She Wrote*) Windom. One of these stories was nominated for the international 2004 SLF Fountain Award for Best Short Story.

These short stories were the foundation for a trilogy of novels published by Airship 27: *Weird Horror Tales, Weird Horror Tales: The Feasting*, and *Weird Horror Tales: Light's End*. With novelists Mel Fox and R.A. Jones, he co-wrote *Global Star*, a tabloid in a world where werewolves and babies born with bowling balls in their stomachs are reality.

He co-wrote *The Equation*, a suspense-thriller about the impending financial collapse of America, with R. A. Jones.

Airship 27 also published Vance's novel, *Young Nemo and the Black Knights* about Jules Vern's Captain Nemo as a young man of eighteen years of age. Vance's weekly comics review column, *Suspended Animation*, was continuously published for more than twenty years in fanzines, newspapers, and on over eighty websites. At its peak, it was read by approximately 4,000,000 readers a year. It was the longest, continuously published, comics review column in the world.

In his career, he worked in newspapers for twenty-two years as an editor, writer and advertising manager, creating three successful newspaper magazines. He also worked as an advertising copy writer, journalist, novelist, historian, graphic designer, in public relations, as a grant writer, cartoonist and columnist. Vance also created the Oklahoma Cartoonists Collection housed in the Toy and Action Figure Museum in Pauls Valley, Oklahoma, and was a keynote speaker at the "Uncanny Adventures of Okie Cartoonists" exhibit at the Oklahoma Historical Museum in Oklahoma City. He is a Christian

COVER ARTIST

TED HAMMOND - is a Canadian artist who has been creating amazing art for over twenty years. His work has appeared in magazines, ads, books and graphic novels just to name a few. Go to (www.tedhammond.com) to contact him and check out more of his work!

INTERIOR ILLUSTRATOR

GREG KEYZER - "Greg K.", is an illustrator, comic illustrator, and cartoonist. Attending The Art Institute of Charlotte, he studied storyboarding and graphic design. His first love being comics, he created a system of producing works combining traditional pen-and-ink with digital mediums. He is currently working on *SidekiX*, a creator-owned work, to be presented soon in multiple formats. See examples of this and other work online at www.freelanced.com/comic.

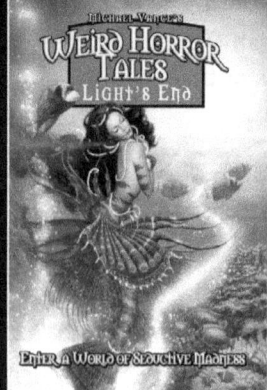

WELCOME TO NOCTURNE, FLORIDA

There has always been something strange about Nocturne, Florida—the City That Lives by Night, It is an entertainment nexus luring tourists from around the world to its nightclubs, music venues and other, more adult entertainment establishments. But there is a darker side to the city which these carefree revelers never see—one of dark doings, violence and eldritch evil.

Now a new sinister force threatens Nocturne and only a handful of unique, gifted beings can protect the city's innocent.

Nightbreaker: a readio star turned vigilante, he exists in a strange limbo world. The beautiful *Dreamcatcher*: who bends all magic to her will. The mysterious *Ferryman*: a living conduit to the world beyond! And their leader: *Black Talon*:the embodiment of the unfettered fury of the African Veld...staling a jungle of concrete and glass.

Together they are *The Shadow Legion*, a secret alliance of mystery men and women who battle the fantastic threats that can tear apart the metropolis they call home!

Their saga begins here in "New Roads To Hell," a gripping novel by Thomas Deja that reveals the secret origins of *Nighbreaker* and *Ferryman*, and features the menace of Rose Red, a crimson-haird devil with a talent for murder!

PULP FICTION FOR A NEW GENERATION!
FOR AVAILABILITY INFORMATION: AIRSHIP27HANGAR.COM

HORROR HAS A NEW FACE

From the pages of the classic pulps comes the most frightening avenger of them all, the Purple Scar!

The handsome, debonair Dr. Miles Murdoch was a world famous plastic surgeon. His life was the stuff of dreams until it all turned into a heart-wrenching nightmare. Murdoch's brother, a dedicated police officer, is brutally gunned down while on patrol. Before dumping his body into the river, his murderers pour acid over his face as a final act of contempt. When the body washes ashore days later, Officer Murdoch's face is beyond recognition, a scarred, purple visage unlike any horror ever imagined.

It is the sight of this death grimace that transforms Miles Murdoch into an avenging angel. Vowing to bring justice to those responsible, the skilled surgeon molds a pliable rubber mask from that repulsive, mutilated face; a mask he dons to become the Purple Scar, the scourge of crooks and villains everywhere. He has become the physical embodiment of their worst fears brought to fiendish life.

Airship 27 now presents four brand new adventures of the creepiest pulp hero of them all, *the Purple Scar!*

www.ingramcontent.com/pod-product-compliance
Lightning Source LLC
Chambersburg PA
CBHW071241250626
47163CB00001B/280